For Tim LaPinske —
"A Good story is
Like medicine to my
Bones."
          A. Lincoln
             1840

      Best wishes!

         JN

        3/7/8

NOTES ON MY RECENT ABDUCTION BY A. LINCOLN 1864

A NARRATIVE ACCOUNT OF THE JOHN WILKES BOOTH PLOT TO KIDNAP PRESIDENT LINCOLN

A Novel by

V. A. Herbert

authorHOUSE®

AuthorHouse™
1663 Liberty Drive, Suite 200
Bloomington, IN 47403
www.authorhouse.com
Phone: 1-800-839-8640

First published by AuthorHouse 1/15/2008

ISBN: 978-1-4343-4093-1 (sc)
ISBN: 978-1-4343-5255-2 (hc)

Library of Congress Control Number: 2007907595

Printed in the United States of America
Bloomington, Indiana

This book is printed on acid-free paper.

For
Mom and Dad

INTRODUCTION

This is a work of fiction, inspired by an historical truth. John Wilkes Booth had organized a gang of men who planned to kidnap President Lincoln in 1864 or 1865 in order to bring the Civil War to an end and allow the Southern Secessionists to prevail. That would have resulted in two nations: The United States of America (USA), and the Confederate States of America (CSA).

For reasons known only to Booth he abandoned the kidnapping plot in the early spring of 1865 and decided suddenly, on Good Friday April 14, 1865, to assassinate the President, five days after the Civil War ended at Appomattox Courthouse, Virginia, where Lee surrendered to Grant.

No one knows what would have happened had Booth gone ahead with the kidnapping. Although it is impossible to believe that it would have altered the war between the states it might have altered the long, bitter, race-driven Reconstruction Era that followed.

It is in my mind more than merely conceivable that we would be living in a far better America today had John Wilkes Booth never been born.

Had Abraham Lincoln been allowed to complete his second term in office it seems likely that he would have found ways and means of settling differences and reconstructing the South in a spirit of generosity and genuine understanding.

V. A. Herbert
March, 2007

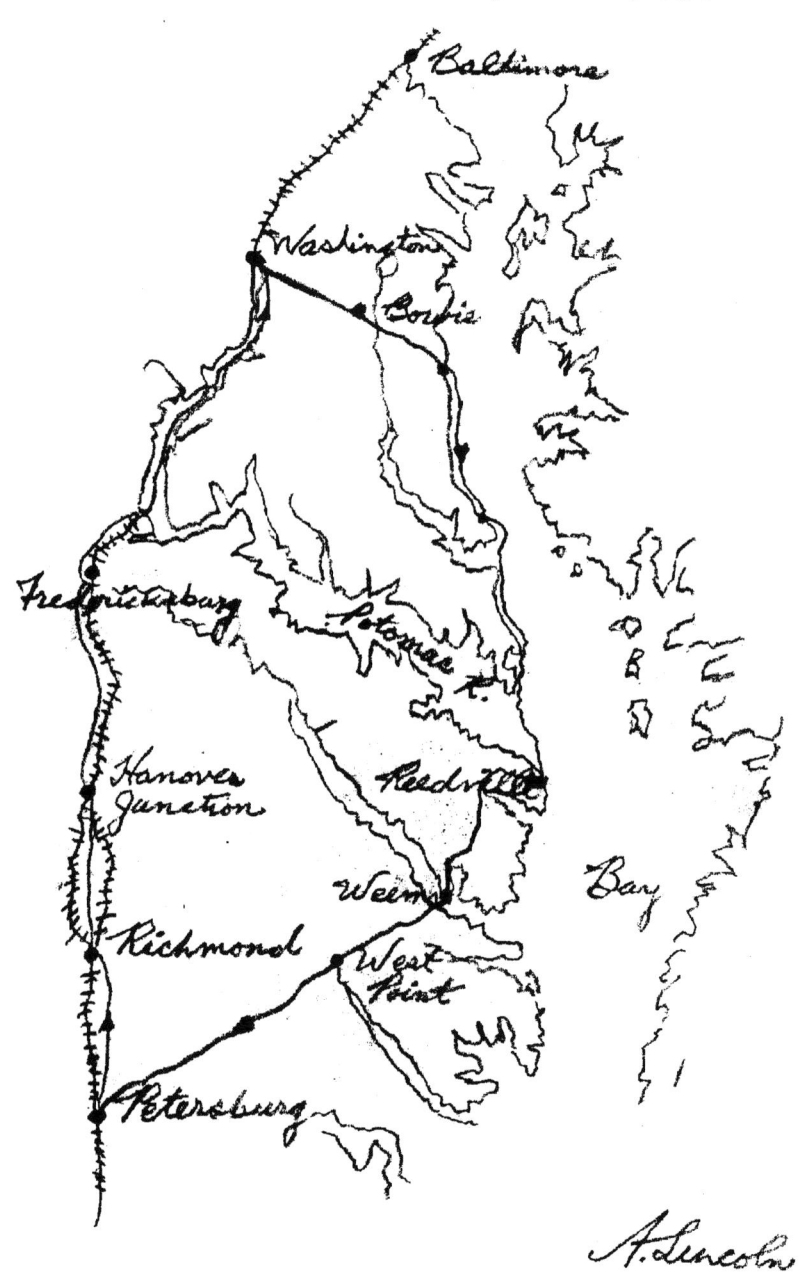

This is where I was
March 31 - April 29, 1864

Baltimore

Washington

Bowis

Fredericksburg

Potomac R.

Hanover Junction

Reedville

Weems

Richmond

West Point

Bay

Petersburg

A. Lincoln

PROLOGUE

Over a period of several months in 1864, while the Civil War still raged on in Virginia, Tennessee and Georgia, John Wilkes Booth, a handsome well-known Shakespearean actor recruited several men who were in agreement that it would be in the South's best interest to sever the head of the snake that was trying to sever them, by kidnapping President Abraham Lincoln. Opponents of the anti-slavery movement, and Lincoln haters, had plotted to kill him in Baltimore, before he could be inaugurated as the 16th President of the United States on March 4, 1861. But they failed. They were outwitted.

With virtually no secret service protection, not at all like heads of state have come to expect all over the world today, the American presidency was an open book, a perpetual open house. People, all kinds of people, were able to enter the Executive Mansion anytime and did, to meet the President or his wife, or ask for a job or favor.

It would not have been difficult to kidnap him. Any of them. It was only a matter of when and where, and if he had to be physically overcome, or coerced in some way.

After that it gets difficult. What do you do with a 6'4" man with a thick black beard, widely recognized by children and adults alike? How do you keep him alive? After all someone has to be responsible. You just can't let him wander about. And how do you collect the ransom? When, how does anyone, or office, or agency say we want you to do this or that, and we will give him back to you? And of equal or greater importance is what does the victim do all this time? How does he handle himself? Whine? Cry? Grovel? Cooperate? Or try calmly to maintain his dignity, integrity, and forbearance despite his caste, even though it may cost him his life.

Fortunately, perhaps because of these and countless other issues and questions, political kidnapping has never been a popular activity, anywhere.

This is the story of what might have happened had President Lincoln been kidnapped by John Wilkes Booth and his gang in the spring of 1864.

Members of Booth's gang included Lewis Powell, David Herold, George Atzerodt, Dr. Samuel A. Mudd, Samuel Arnold, Michael O'Laughlen and John H. Surratt, Jr. You are about to meet some of them.

THURSDAY, MARCH 31, 1864

There was nothing unusual about this day up to the time when your mother and I decided to ride out into the country. The weather was reasonably warm and trees were beginning to show their green side. A lovely day for a short ride, if only to escape the dreadful casualty lists that I have been receiving for the past three years.

As usual, I asked for Will Crudge, our faithful driver for many years. He always seemed to know the best roads to follow and had an excellent way with our team of horses.

Old Will, whom everyone addressed as Mr. Crudge, was a short thin man, always dressed in a black suit, white shirt and cravat. A distinguished looking gentleman with prematurely white hair, Mr. Crudge never failed to have a good story about one or more of the presidents he knew from years past. Mrs. Lincoln and I used to enjoy having dinner with him in the Executive Mansion. Everyone liked Will, including the horses. President Andrew Jackson hired him as a favor to a friend in 1830, and he served continuously from that time, ten presidents including me.

We left the Executive Mansion about 1 o'clock, over New York Avenue, then north, on 7th street, calculating that the sun would have warmed the land a bit and cleansed the air for a refreshing drive. If I seem a little slow in getting to the point boys, it's because I am still in a state of disbelief. I find it hard to believe that the good Lord spared me from all that I have heard and witnessed during the past few weeks.

Please forgive my laxity and ineptitude in preparing this post mortem account of your father's experience with forces so evil they are hard to describe.

Several minutes passed pleasantly before we reached the soldiers' home where we shared so many happy hours with the veterans and the Secretary of War Mr. Stanton, and his Missus, Ellen Stanton. As we crossed over into Maryland and the town of Silver Spring, Mrs. Lincoln became a little restless. "Now you know how they feel about you up here, my dear," she said. Just as I was about to tell her not to worry, Mr. Crudge turned our carriage east and began to slow down. He was about to tell us something when we all were completely surprised by three or four men in two fancy carriages. One of the men, whom I thought I recognized as the famous actor John Wilkes Booth, started shouting orders at the others and at Mr. Crudge. My wife started crying, "Oh Abe, Oh Abe". I thought she was going to faint.

Then Booth shouted at me, "Step down you royal monster and be quick about it." As calmly as I could under the circumstances, I replied that I would not leave my wife unprotected. "You are making a terrible mistake, Mr. Booth, if that in fact is who you are. I have no intention of alighting from this carriage."

While I spoke as if in command, it fell on unhearing ears.

"You are correct, sir. I am John Wilkes Booth. And, you need not fear for your wife's protection. I will have one of my men take Mrs. Lincoln back to the Executive Mansion."

"That is not acceptable," I replied. " We shall remain together until we understand what is going on here. Now, kindly remove your carriage and let us pass. We shall hear no more of this commotion and shall continue on at our pleasure."

"Never," Booth shouted, reaching in his black silk jacket. And, before I could say anything more, Booth stepped closer to me and Mrs. Lincoln, pointed a pistol at Mr. Crudge, and shot him dead.

Horror stricken, your mother shouted, "Oh God, Abe, go with him, go, please. I do not want this evil to fall on you, all for me. Please, I'll be all right. Do as he says."

"I'm sorry my darling, but I'm not going to leave you alone." No sooner than I spoke, Booth came closer still and threatened to shoot Mrs. Lincoln, too. I had to choose.

"We are apparently dealing with a madman, my darling, and so I will go with them and pray to God they will return you safely." With that, I stepped over Mr. Crudge's body and jumped to the ground.

One of the gang members immediately took my place and, as if rehearsed, pushed Mr. Crudge off the carriage as he turned it around and headed back the way we had come. Sorrowfully, I watched as the buggy disappeared, your mother crying and wailing loudly all the while.

"What in God's name is this all about Booth?" I demanded at the top of my voice. "I am the President of the United States of America, engaged in a massive civil conflict that is costing the lives of thousands of men. How dare you confront me and my beloved wife under these abhorrent circumstances? What is your business, sir?"

But, while I spoke, I could see a black glass-enclosed funeral hearse approaching us. I thought the end was near. Very quickly and efficiently, with nothing more said, some members of Booth's gang opened the door and revealed a large black coffin.

Without ado, I was gagged and bound, then placed in the coffin. One of the men said there were breathing holes and to remain still. They then put a board over me and what I guessed was a body, probably that of Mr. Crudge. Still nothing more was said and the hearse began to move.

All of this boys, from the moment Booth first stopped us, took place within a matter of a few minutes. This deed, I reckoned it to be a kidnap, was clearly well thought out and by very determined people. For what purpose, I knew not. But, I must admit, I began to feel a bit more confident that Mrs. Lincoln would be returned home safely. A morbid fear of being confined in a dark tightly enclosed space swept over me as I kept testing my lungs, and hoping that nothing would block the air holes on which my life depended. I tried not to think of it as being buried alive, but I could not escape the fear.

We had not moved very far before I began to hear rain falling and the drivers beginning to laugh and talk although I could not hear what they said. Then, the laughter stopped and I could clearly hear loud cursing. This continued for a few minutes as the horses slowed down and then stopped.

Apparently, we had reached a checkpoint maintained by federal troops, or a contingent of federal troops had decided to stop traffic moving north for some reason.

The rain continued, hard falling rain - enough to delay movement on the road north to Columbia, and this was what brought on the storm of abuse from the drivers. They were about to be questioned by the Federal Military Police, searching for deserters from the Army of the Potomac. One of the drivers told me to remain still or a lot of people would soon die.

I decided to cooperate but hoped, nonetheless, that our soldiers would search diligently. Such was not to happen. They opened the casket, but seeing a dead body assumed that it was on its way to a cemetery, and quickly left the hearse, chuckling about how comfortable the cadaver looked compared to everyone else, soaked by the rain.

We moved on then at a faster pace, to where I knew not. Hours went by during which I probably fell asleep. The rain had stopped. Now the road was rough, as on a trail. The gag cloth was too tight and my hands and arms ached, so I tried to go back to sleep. But it was too hot and I felt pain from lying too long in the same cramped position. I thought of you both, and Willie, and your mother. And prayed deeply that all of you were safe and protected. I also gave thought to what might come of this abduction. Was I to be ransomed? That did not seem to make much sense there being John Wilkes Booth's involvement. But what? Was it possible they expected the Union to stop the war? Or ameliorate? Or negotiate?

Having fallen asleep again, I was awakened by a gang member who removed my gag and the ropes binding my hands and feet. I was very unsteady, of course, but determined to remain as dignified as possible. These people had to realize they were dealing with the Head of State, and although I personally consider myself an ordinary human being of humble origin and character, I could not allow these brigands in the act of transgressing on our laws and constitution to succeed in ignoring the presidency. It was necessary for me therefore, to carry on as the President, always.

It was dark and by my pocket watch, 5 o'clock. A gang member said it was night and asked me if I wanted some bacon and beans. He said they would continue on after a bit but gave no reply when asked where they intended to take me.

The gang member who did most of the talking was a young man named John Surratt, Jr. The other man, George Atzerodt was a Prussian immigrant, about ten years older than Surratt. Mr. Atzerodt was supposed to be a good boatman, especially familiar with the Potomac River, but I have reason to question that, which I will get to later. He spoke with a heavy accent and liked to drink large amounts of liquor at one sitting. He said he had been a carriage painter in Port Tobacco, Maryland.

Mr. Surratt lived with his mother here, in Washington City. He had been a courier for the Confederates before meeting up with Booth. A wily, energetic, fellow of nineteen or twenty, John Surratt had worked for an express company, and knew the back roads of southern Maryland and eastern Virginia. An interesting man, Mr. Surratt is one of the cleverest, most innovative men I have ever known.

Finally, I was told to lie back in the coffin and remain quiet, that if I behaved they would allow me to sit up and stretch. The black curtains were drawn and I was not to look out.

FRIDAY, APRIL 1, 1864

We were back on the road in several minutes and I was, admittedly, somewhat more comfortable. The drivers did very little talking so once again I tried to get some sleep. We stopped three or four more times, but I may have slept through one or more before the sun rose and we stopped at what I now believe was a tavern, probably in Bowie, Maryland, from what I overheard John say.

After giving me a few raw eggs, a jug of water and an empty bucket, John told me they were going to get some rest and ordered me to stay out of sight or my loved ones would pay the price. I did not know exactly what he meant by that, but felt it best to obey under the circumstances.

Samuel Arnold, the Booth gang member who was assigned the task of returning Mrs. Lincoln to the Executive Mansion apparently decided at the last minute, that caution was called for as he drove down New York Avenue with Mrs. Lincoln still crying and yelling loudly.

"They have taken my husband captive! Your Father Abraham is gone! Someone must help….the President has been kidnapped!"

Arnold drove the carriage into Lafayette Square immediately facing the Executive Mansion told Mrs. Lincoln he could go no further and left.

As she continued screaming, people gathered around the carriage and, having recognized her, tried to calm her. Finally someone said a doctor ought to be called, or perhaps the Vice President or Mr. Stanton the Secretary of War or Tad the president's youngest son. A physician did appear shortly and after patient questioning, said that Mr. Stanton should be called at once and that he, Doctor Jonas Meek, would take Mrs. Lincoln to the Executive Mansion in his carriage.

"Please have Mr. Stanton meet us there." He told the crowd, "It's very important. The President's life may be in danger."

Edwin Stanton was an attorney, and a very close and trusted friend of the President. It was Stanton who more than anyone else kept the war on an even keel, never failing the President as Commander in Chief to pursue people and policies that would serve the nation best. A man of substance and cogent intelligence, Stanton always acted in the President's best interest. And this was no time to fail although he knew he had little to go on.

He thought at first that the kidnappers would take their hostage to Baltimore or Columbia. But, why Maryland? Even though it was a hotbed of discontent and outspoken southern sympathy, if this hostile act had anything to do with the war then Abe Lincoln would wind up in the South, Virginia most likely. Perhaps even further south. So Stanton reasoned Baltimore is only a clever diversion. The real destination is south of us not north.

The first telegraph Stanton sent out went to John Kennedy, Chief of Police in New York City. In it he asked for several detectives to be sent to Washington to help locate President Lincoln and arrest Mr. John Wilkes Booth. He followed that with two more telegraph messages to Brigadier General Morris, Commanding District of Baltimore and Lieutenant General Grant, in the field near Fredericksburg, Virginia. In each message he told the story of how and where the President was captured, and demanded that John Wilkes Booth be taken alive as soon as possible. Let no man or expense stand in the way.

Stanton ordered Morris to begin an intensive search for the President throughout southern Maryland and, in particular, towns and villages along Chesapeake Bay, anywhere a boat could be launched quietly and privately. He ordered Grant to do the same in Virginia forthwith.

Well I did look out. Carefully I peeked between the heavy curtains and enjoyed for a bit the wonderful morning sunlight. I began to think about the possibility of escape but knew that the door was locked, and the people I would expect to help me flee to safety might not be all that willing to assist in view of their southern leanings. I decided to await a better opportunity to leave their custody. Perhaps some Federal troops would come to my rescue before long. Such hopes were always vitiated somewhat by my thoughts of your safety and of your mother's well being. I wanted no harm to come to any of you. This was a problem best handled by the Federal Government.

My pocket watch indicated 10 o'clock as I gazed at it for some time. It was a beautiful timepiece, a Swiss movement made by Baume & Mercier, given to me by Mrs. Lincoln and you boys, including Willie of course, on March 4, 1861 the day I was inaugurated and became the 16th President of the United States. It was a thoughtful gift which still reminds me of that day and of all of you every time I reach for my solid silver timepiece and the simple but loving inscription:

President Abraham Lincoln
"We love our Father Abraham"
Bob, Eddie, Willie & Tad
Mary
March 4, 1861

Time passed slowly indeed and the heat of the day was difficult to endure when finally Mr. Atzerodt opened the door, said we were moving on and closed the door quickly. I could understand why since the body of Mr. Crudge was lying on the floor of the hearse beside me and had begun to emit a foul odor. Time and the direct heat of the sun were playing no favorites.

Slowly but steadily the horses pulled the hearse along rough, unimproved roads toward I knew not where. I passed the time by going back through my life. Where was I on March 31, 1854? What did I do, what was I thinking? Who were my friends and associates then? What could or should I have done differently? Then, where was I on March 31, 1844? Same thing, an interesting way to pass the time and take stock.

I kept this up until I got back to as far as my memory would allow, March 31, 1814. I can go back further, not quite to 1809 when I was born, but those memories seem to stand by themselves. It is difficult to connect them to anything except childhood. Then after things got a little repetitious and boring I tried to sleep and I suppose I did. The door opened suddenly and I could feel the night air. I could also hear water. A lot of water. Steady uninterrupted fast flowing water. Surratt would not tell me what it was but I knew it almost had to be the Chesapeake. It was midnight.

SATURDAY, APRIL 2, 1864

From what I gathered by listening attentively we were lost. The farm which we were supposed to reach by this time did not fit the specifications as delineated by whomever planned this crime, presumably John Wilkes Booth. Both Surratt and Atzerodt, my very tired drivers, made a serious effort to search for a dock and boat but nothing of the kind could be found.

"You want to help us look?" Surratt asked me at one point, to which I replied "Only if you both agree to sail and leave me behind." Nothing more was said but they continued looking and conferring quietly at a distance.

The night was cold and I too was rather tired. I could of course see as well as hear the water, and wondered if my captors might possibly think of unhitching the horses and floating the hearse down the bay. Had they thought of it, it must have been ruled out as too fatuous to contemplate.

I wrapped myself in the blanket I retrieved from my coffin and walked about for some exercise, and tried to enjoy the nighttime air and the pleasant music of the bay as it flowed gently by. I thought about jumping in and letting the currents carry me south but I ruled that one out also as too hazardous, although I must admit the idea had some merit if I could have found a log or something I could cling to on a watery journey to safety. Or should I say danger?

I noticed that Mr. Surratt had wandered down the bay shore, out of sight, and thought he must be trying to locate the proper place where we should be by now, or at least a boat that could be used to carry us away. I decided to return to my casket and get some more sleep. It was almost 3 a.m.

I was awake and standing outside the wagon at 7 a.m. when Surratt made an appearance from the north. He later told me that he thought it would make more sense to float a boat with the current rather than against it, in the event he found a boat. He didn't think it would be a good idea for three men to be seen walking along the banks of the bay in street clothes should he find a boat downstream.

At least he has a brain, I thought. But, I chose not to comment since the timing was not yet right to try to engage him in conversation.

He told me to leave nothing behind. We would abandon the hearse and horses which once again I let pass without comment. I knew that sooner or later someone would discover the tram and ultimately, perhaps my trail, which is why I left my cherished pocket watch carefully hidden in Mr. Crudge's vest pocket.

Shocked by Stanton's telegram, General Morris gathered his staff and maps of Maryland's western shore. He said it would be impossible to search the eastern shoreline, there being too many inlets and places to hide.

Starting near Fort McHenry, in the immediate Baltimore City area, and extending south all the way to Point Lookout at the south westernmost tip of the Maryland peninsula in St. Mary's County, every foot of land and water along Chesapeake Bay would be searched for President Lincoln or any evidence that he had been there. And this effort was to begin now with a total of 100 men assigned to four special platoons to search the craggy 100 mile coastline. The Non-Commissioned Officer in charge of each platoon was ordered to report his findings every day by special courier.

General Grant telegraphed his desire and intent to cooperate in a thorough search of the 260 mile coastline of Virginia, from Aquia Landing to Newport News, and up and down every river in between, but said he would need more men to accomplish the task. Battles which he could foresee would consume all the forces at his command.

Stanton replied that 300 men including officers and NCO's would be entrained from Washington this very day.

Stanton also met with Admiral David Porter, Chief of the Washington Naval District, to request urgent U. S. Navy activity on Chesapeake Bay and environs as far south as Fort Story, on Cape Henry, where the bay meets the Atlantic Ocean.

To date there were no leads as to the missing President other than what could be provided by Mrs. Lincoln, but as he sat in his office, pencil in hand, pondering the possibilities, a message arrived from Vice President Hamlin that said a letter from the kidnappers had just been received. Hannibal Hamlin was pacing the floor of his office when Stanton arrived flush from his hurried trip upon hearing the news. "Who signed the letter?" he gasped, and upon hearing that it was John Wilkes Booth seemed to stop breathing. He stared at the letter on Hamlin's desk for the longest time, then "What inconceivable connection could exist between Abe Lincoln and Booth?" Hamlin stopped pacing, sat at his desk and stared ahead. "None that I know of. None" he said, handing the letter to the Secretary of War. "But as you can see, Mr. Stanton, we have a very serious problem, and I'm going to need all the help you can give me."

"Indeed, sir you need not fear any lack of complete cooperation on my part or from the Army or Navy. I have already given orders to undertake an exhaustive search of key sections of Maryland and Virginia in a major effort to find my dear friend, our President. Now let me read this letter."

Holding the letter now and looking at it but not reading it, Edwin McMasters Stanton appeared to be in a state of shock. For several minutes, he held the letter as his eyes watered and hands began to tremble. Mr. Hamlin sat still and watched. "I can't do it. You read it, aloud."

Hamlin began, "It is addressed to me of course on letterhead stationery dated March 31, 1864."

> "Mr. Hamlin, this is to inform you that President Abraham Lincoln is in our custody and is well and uninjured. I must caution you and your compatriots, however, that these conditions may change for better or worse, depending for the most part on how you and your government respond to our demands, which we believe to be reasonable and practical. Thus, the life of your President impends upon whichever action you command.
>
> It is in your hands, my dear sir, so you must assume the responsibility. We demand the immediate cessation of all military activity by the Armed Forces of the United States of America, a withdrawal of all such forces to their native Union States, a guarantee that such forces will not be reactivated, and that the Confederate States of America be recognized in appropriate U. S. congressional legislation signed by you into law. These demands are non-negotiable and must be accepted and acted upon to completion by the end of April, 1864.
>
> Your Humble Servant and Political Savior,
> John Wilkes Booth."

Stanton stood as soon as the letter ended. "By God" he swore, "We'll hang that faker so high a balloon wouldn't reach him. Or perhaps we can hang him from the balloon."

Distraught almost beyond endurance, his long brown jacket flapping, he strode quickly from the room saying nothing to the Vice President or the few who had collected outside the office. Edwin Stanton was mad as hell. He went directly to Major General Henry Halleck the Army Chief of Staff.

"Halleck by God we've got to find the President. I don't trust anyone else to continue fighting these seditious sons…, these traitors to our flag. We just received word from them that they have Lincoln and are threatening to harm or kill him if we don't quit the war. The gall, the unmitigated gall of that devil, that rascal, John Wilkes Booth. Who in God's name does he think he is? Our political savior he says. Unforgivable. Extortion, blackmail, kidnap, treason. This crime, in his hand, knows no greater evil Halleck. We must find the President! And, soon!"

Newspapers around the country had been following and printing the story of the kidnapping since word was first received upon Mary Todd Lincoln's hysterical return to the Executive Mansion via Lafayette Square on March 31st.

News boys in the streets of Washington could be heard shouting news of death threats and kidnappers' demands. "Booth, the famous actor, has kidnapped President Lincoln!" they cried.

"Secretary Stanton went on, "I believe we need to form several special teams of men and some women to infiltrate and circulate amongst their peers in Maryland and Virginia, initially, in their own clothes of course. No uniforms, or guns, or Federal identification on them. These people should be volunteers; intelligent, dedicated, eager secret service agents who can acquire useful information that we can act on to free the President. Do you believe you can put such a force together?"

"I understand sir," Halleck answered. "It will be done."

"Excellent. And you can use the nine detectives who just arrived from New York City" Stanton said.

As he rose to leave, "Give them all the money you can General, and tell them to communicate with me directly if you will. I must know if this plan has any merit. If these secret agents can seduce or bribe any Southerners to cooperate in the search, so much the better. I don't care who we corrupt and keep in mind, a Confederate dollar is now only worth a Yankee nickel. The mission is to save Mr. Lincoln's life and further the cause of Union solidarity. We must win this war!"

Henry Halleck was too overcome with emotion and the sudden abrupt orders from his boss to find qualified people on short notice to act as spies in enemy territory. How and where am I to find these people he wondered? And a lot of them. He, Halleck, had just won promotion to Chief of Staff hardly two years ago despite George McClellan's longing for the job. Now once again he had to deliver. And John Wilkes Booth? General Halleck remembered that he had forgotten to ask Stanton about that. What was Booth doing in this? What were his demands? How much time did the North have to save the Union and Mr. Lincoln?

In the dim light I could see an old, terribly weathered sailboat with a narrow hull about ten feet long. My first thought was that three men on this skiff would be a crowd and very uncomfortable.

"The best I could do" Mr. Surratt said as he threw my blanket and pillow aboard. "No doubt the owner will miss it but I don't think we will when this journey is over" he continued. "I'm sure it's not the boat we were supposed to have but it will have to do."

'We can't wait for dawn and start asking questions. We've got to move on. So, get on the boat, Mr. President" he said sarcastically, "and we'll push off."

We pushed the light boat off shore with a long pole that was on the vessel when we boarded and tried to stay close to shore as the current carried us south, and the sun rose to greet us. We could not all three of us stretch out at the same time but at least there was no coffin or body to concern me.

As we floated down Chesapeake Bay constantly poling on the port side to keep from sailing too far out, we watched the farms and beach fronts pass rather quickly. It must have occurred to Surratt and Atzerodt as it certainly did to me that people on shore and on other boats were bound to see us and possibly identify me. But, that obviously didn't bother either of them for they made no effort to conceal my features. After a while I began to wave back when now and then some folks, especially children, waved at us. Since I was not told to stop I actually began to enjoy the friendly smiles and shouts we experienced along the way. I wondered if the word of my voyage would ever get back to the Capitol or to anyone who might be searching for me. This being Maryland however I dismissed the idea as I'm sure my captors did too. These people were Southern sympathizers after all, not likely to report my sudden appearance on a small boat in their bay on a chilly day in early April. "Does not appear out of the ordinary for Abe Lincoln to do something like that" they would say. "He's just a baboon you know."

Thirst and hunger finally forced us to find a suitable place to stop which we did about noon, the sun being directly overhead. What I now know as Plum Point, Maryland, proved to be a fine place for fresh water seafarers to disembark and replenish bodies and souls. Their souls not mine. I was told to stay on the boat but was never alone.

After an hour or so respite we started out again, but somewhat against the wind on what had become a very chilly day. We had no choice but to suffer and pole, pole and suffer. And I had my share of both.

In a few hours we poled ashore and tried to make camp. Fortunately there were a lot of trees to protect us from the wind, but all of our efforts to catch small game were unsuccessful, so we settled for a few crabs baked in a small rock stove which we were finally able to create and light. Extremely tired we just lay on the ground and fell asleep.

SUNDAY, APRIL 3, 1864

The sun was fairly high and shining brightly in a clear sky when all of us awoke at about the same time. With no food we had to satisfy ourselves with water from the bay using last night's crab shells as a cup. I kept the shells in my pockets.

Before boarding our little sailboat Surratt unfolded a small piece of paper which turned out to be a map of the Maryland and Virginia area we were traversing. From the tip of the Maryland Peninsula which I know now as Point Lookout, I overheard him say we were to cross the Potomac River and continue on down Chesapeake Bay to Hampton, Virginia, to meet up with a man with a carriage and team of horses.

"Unfortunately" Mr. Surratt said, "there ain't no provisions been made for food, so that means," pausing to think carefully about what he planned to do, "means we're going to stay in Maryland and find some food, or cross the Potomac and find some food on the Virginia side. Either way we got to get something to eat or risk starving to death. Now we can't do that Mr. Lincoln can we?" he said with smiling sarcasm. "Why we'd lose the war for sure then. You wouldn't be around to save us."

And that was what this was all about I learned with some finality in just a few well-chosen words. I was going to be used by John Wilkes Booth to stop the war and allow the South to secede.

"Do you believe that Jefferson Davis would feel sorry if I were to starve?" I asked. No reply was forthcoming.

"Let's get on with this" Mr. Surratt ordered suddenly, "We're going to Virginia or out to sea." Whereupon we boarded the boat and set sail for Point Lookout. Like the day before we stayed close to shore and before long got lucky. Some boys were fishing from high rocks and began pelting us with apples. The apples were a little old , some rotting, but floating, meaning we were able to at least have something to ward off starvation. By the time we reached the Potomac River at Point Lookout, the sky had begun to darken. Perhaps that is why we escaped notice by the Federal troops guarding large numbers of Confederate prisoners at Point Lookout. Neither Mr. Surratt nor I knew of this until we had long passed the U. S. fort there. As apprehensive as I was about crossing the Potomac in such a small boat with two others in squally circumstances, I had no alternative but to continue on with my captors.

I suggested we stop here at the point and wait for the storm to pass and winds to subside but Surratt would not hear of it. "We're going to be late in arriving at our final destination as it is and I don't want to make it any worse. We are going to cross to Virginia now and get some hospitality as soon as we arrive. A little trouble ain't going to stop us, right Mr. Lincoln?"

I just looked at him and smiled.

But it would be the last smile for a long time. The next twenty four hours will always be among the most miserable I have ever experienced.

We entered the river as it began to rain lightly at first, then heavily. Combined with strong gusts of wind and low temperature, what would have been about a ten mile difficult crossing became a much longer treacherous voyage.

Fighting constantly for hours without oars or even a paddle or bailing bucket, simply trying to avoid overturning, we all became limp from utter exhaustion and gave up. Choppy water, fast moving currents and remorseless rain had defeated us. And, as the storm continued to suck all of our life forces away and I felt that we had reached the nadir, lightning flashed and a high wave of water threw us into a trough and overturned us. We flayed about, desperately trying to grab hold of the boat and climb back in. I think I saved Surratt from drowning because as I learned later, neither he nor Atzerodt could swim. Mr. Atzerodt disappeared. We looked and shouted from the boat but could not find him. We bailed water frantically by soaking our trousers and wringing them dry.

Then we lay prostrate, gripping the hand rails and each other, praying loudly and proudly. It was awful. An almost full moon amid fast moving clouds, and loud strikes of lightning revealed an angry river, its high wet and cold choppy waves crashing over us, and about us.

> *Yeah, though I walk through the Valley of the Shadow of Death, I will fear no evil: for thou art with me; thy rod and thy staff they comfort me. God will redeem my soul from the power of the grave; for He shall receive me.*

Strangely we must have each fallen asleep at some point despite all that was happening about us.

Hours later I was awakened by Mr. Surratt, who thanked me for saving his life and expressing his deep sorrow for having been responsible for Atzerodt's presumed drowning. "You're a good man Mr. Lincoln," he told me with a wistful smile. "I hope that I may be able to return the favor some day but know not how without violating my word of honor. I did after all promise Mr. Booth that I would carry out this mission according to his plan, and I intend to honor my commitment."

Although the sun was completely obscured by a cloud cover the river was calm once again and the rain had stopped. No land could be seen in any direction nor any boats that might help us navigate. We just sat and meditated for a bit before I gently asked Mr. Surratt if he thought Mrs. Lincoln would be returned home safely. He assured me that she would because the plan in no way involved her or our children.

"The plan calls for me to deliver you to a certain private home in Petersburg by April 7, and that's supposed to allow some time for unforeseen problems and trouble. We may be able to get there by then but it seems less likely as we go on."

"Why April 7?"

"No special reason that I know of. I know they want to get the North to quit and maybe the sooner they have you in Petersburg, the sooner we can end the war."

"I don't understand why my presence in Petersburg or anywhere for that matter, would help end the war any sooner. What do you think they plan to do with me?"

"I don't know Mr. Lincoln. I have no knowledge of that part of the plan. Maybe they want to send them something that belongs to you to prove you are in their control, or are still alive and well."

"Well I suppose that ought to be encouraging but I can conceive of something more sinister that they might want to do, in order to shorten or attempt to shorten the war."

"Such as?"

"Such as torture or perhaps the removal of certain body parts that would frighten the people up North and perhaps force the Union to concede. Do you think that is possible or likely?"

"No. Most emphatically, no. Should anyone suggest that or attempt to do that, I know that I would object and fight that scheme. I believe that others would agree with me."

"That is encouraging John" I said realizing that I had made some progress toward developing a rapport with a loyal Booth conspirator, and that might help alleviate the probability, which I had foreseen by that time, of being the principal means by which Booth and his cohorts planned to intimidate Vice President Hamlin and the Congress. Cutting off body parts and sending them North with accompanying photographs would have a devastating affect on Union morale, and could result in enough public pressure to force the House of Representatives to stop funding our military forces. A gruesome, hideous way to act, but some people know no limits when it comes to achieving their personal objectives.

Dimly, far ahead of us as we drifted down the bay, we could see a thin slice of land on the horizon, but we could also see that we were far enough out on the bay to miss landfall unless we could somehow maneuver the boat closer to shore. We began to lean to starboard and shift our bodies from upright positions to extreme starboard, rhythmically and to a strong beat, in order to steer toward shore. One two three turn! One two three turn! One two three turn! I can still feel that urgency, and how we felt when we knew that it was indeed the way, probably the only way, to reach land and food.

It was not without great trepidation that we knew what the alternatives to reaching land now would impose. We would be out in the bay somewhere with very little hope of terra firma anywhere until we were both too weak to survive.

Since the rudder in our little boat which we had begun to call The Mayflower Two didn't seem to work well, I decided to remove my shoes and my soaking wet clothes in order to get in the water and push the boat toward shore. It was cold but by kicking my legs as fast as I could, we seemed to make some progress. When John started to remove his clothes, I asked him to stay in the boat and continue rocking. I would need some help getting back in. Each time I was in the river I tried to scratch my name on the hull of the boat with my shells, in the forlorn hope that someone might find it someday and know that I was here.

The night passed slowly as I climbed in and out of the boat a number of times in a vain attempt to warm up a bit before getting back into the water. Although I am a born pessimist, I was confident that we would make shore if I could find the strength to keep paddling. The sun was beginning to burn through the clouded sky and gave us more hope. The area appeared marshy with mangroves but Surratt stood and pointed toward solid ground. "At last, thanks be to God" I said aloud, "The Mayflower has landed safely." We were on land once again and slept the rest of the day.

MONDAY, APRIL 4, 1864

While Lincoln and John were sleeping Edwin Stanton was pounding his fist on General Halleck's desk demanding action. A telegraph message had been received from Baltimore but failed to provide enough information.

Tuesday, April 4, 1864
Secretary of War
Edwin M. Stanton
Washington City

My men report several sightings of three men in a small boat hugging Maryland shoreline going south on Chesapeake Bay. To some of the witnesses one of the men appears to resemble the President.

> Will keep you informed.
> Morris

"Where are the facts General? When were they seen? What days? Where were they last seen? When? Good Lord man, we've got to know all of the details. Telegraph Morris and have him wire an immediate reply."

"And now General let us talk about how our people are going to infiltrate behind the lines in Virginia. I have met with the New York detectives who tell me that money will be a problem. That's certainly no secret but it would introduce trouble if our people use Northern money exclusively. So the detectives recommend we use gold. That probably makes the most sense because it will pass anywhere and the recipient is not likely to talk about it.

"It's also a temptation," Halleck added quickly.

"Nevertheless, ten gold coins, one ounce each, worth a total of about 500 dollars in today's financial markets are only going to weigh ten ounces. Then add two or three hundred in Federal greenbacks."

"It would be perfect for bribery sir if used carefully but carelessness will surely result in their being caught or killed. They are getting hungry down there Mr. Stanton, and would not hesitate to kill a man for gold. I know it is a lot of money. Especially when you consider that a U. S. Army private earns only 13 dollars a month."

"I know that but we've got to act quickly and I don't know that it may already be too late. How can three men in a small boat if that in fact is how they are traveling, how can they possibly cross the Potomac? That's an idiotic plan. Sounds like something an actor like Booth would invent. A fantasy. Belongs in a theatre. Good God Almighty, Lincoln could drown and we'd never know. I have got to see Welles again about the Navy's plans. I think they ought to concentrate on the river. Don't you?"

General Halleck rose from his desk and looked at a wall map behind him. "Well sir even if they manage to cross the river, and there isn't any other practical way around it, it's not going to be easy for them. They'll still be a long way from civilization."

Stanton began pacing back and forth. "It looks like we are going to have to have the Navy take our spies up the Potomac and set them ashore on the Virginia side. That is going to be a high risk venture and I don't know that it can be done. If Lee continues harassing us on that waterway we would have to have an alternative plan. We just cannot count on the U. S. Potomac Flotilla to save us here."

"Well we could have the spies take a boat across the river from the Maryland shore."

"That's an idea Halleck. Good. If the Navy supplies each two man team of spies with a boat the Army can certainly get them and their boats to a few places along the river where they can cross at night, and there won't be any moon on Wednesday. Can you get them there by the 6th?"

"If I can have the boats today I can do it."

"You understand General that all this has to stay secret. Word cannot get out or the entire mission will be compromised."

"I need not be reminded of my duties as an officer and Chief of Staff, Mr. Secretary," Halleck quickly retorted.

Stanton turned and walked away. "Thank you" he said, looking down as he left the room. "I deserved that."

"Oh wait" Stanton said reentering General Halleck's office. "I want you to know that we are offering a reward totaling $200,000 for the safe return of President Lincoln and the arrest of John Wilkes Booth. $150,000 for Mr. Lincoln, $50,000 for Booth. The money has been pledged by various cities and states throughout the country, and I expect more will follow soon. I have ordered 10,000 reward posters and want them to appear everywhere: police stations, barracks, forts, hospitals, railroad stations, taverns, bordellos, anywhere people gather. We must circulate these reward notices. And the rebels should know, too, that they are eligible. Will you help me get these posters up General?"

"You know I will Mr. Secretary. Give me all 10,000 to start."

Shortly after Secretary Stanton reached his office a courier delivered a telegram.

April 4, 1864
Secretary of War
Edwin M. Stanton
Washington City

Boat party with 3 men last seen by some boys late afternoon Sunday, April 2, on shore near village of Ridge, Maryland, about 8 to 10 miles from Lookout Point. Also, another detachment found a large silver pocket watch, belonging to President Lincoln, on the body of a Mr. Crudge, in an abandoned hearse near Churchton, Maryland. We do not know who Crudge is. He died of a gun shot wound. No other details available now.

Will keep you informed.
Morris

TUESDAY, APRIL 5, 1864

We awoke about mid-morning to the happy sounds of big and small birds unseen but all about. Our clothes had dried even as we slept in them but our shoes were still wet and soggy. There were no rocks about so we would not have been able to light a fire even if we had something to cook, which we did not. Surratt had wandered off but returned in a few minutes with a good sized turtle.

"We could make some turtle soup if only we had a fire. If not we'll have to eat this raw if I can break his shell."

"He will fit in the boat if we cannot do that," I suggested hoping somehow that we would not have to eat raw turtle.

"Well let's get started" he said at last. "I found something we can use as a pole to get out of this swamp."

Sticking close to the shore we rounded Smith Point and stopped at the tiny rural settlement of Reedville, Virginia, close to noon. Rather than leave me in the boat alone, John asked me to join him as we walked toward a little shed which also passed as a store. The storekeeper, an older gentleman who called himself James Mitchin welcomed us with big brown eyes that stared at me with fear and bewilderment. Surratt had asked me to try to stay back a bit and out of sight but it was to no avail. My height and scrawny features were easily recognizable even in this little place far removed from Washington or Richmond.

Mr. Mitchin didn't say a word. Just stared trying to decide how to handle this completely unexpected and highly unusual advent which he would no doubt be describing for the rest of his life, so I decided to introduce myself. "My name is Abe Lincoln Mr. Mitchin. This other gentleman and I are just passing through and are very hungry. What can you do for us by way of food and drink?"

Mr. Mitchin came a little closer and shook my hand not paying any attention to what I had just said.

"You know the newspapers are looking for you Mr. Lincoln" he said excitedly. "They say you've been kidnapped by that actor feller, you know, John Wilkes Booth. Are you kidnapped?" Mitchin squinted and stood close as I tried to compose an answer that would satisfy him and Mr. Surratt, who stood by my side silently.

"Well everyone has a right to their own opinion Mr. Mitchin, even newspapers. But at the moment I feel perfectly safe with my friend here, and if only we can get something to eat I'm sure I'll feel even better. Now what do you have to eat?"

Mr. Mitchin relaxed a bit as he backed off and said he had some nice sausage. "I guess I could cook you up some eggs too if you can wait a few minutes." We laughed and said, "We'll wait."

For some reason I hadn't thought about payment for all the food we ate, which was quite ample, until Surratt pulled a small black leather bag from his pocket and laid a gold coin on a box. It turned out to be more than enough and Mr. Mitchin was obviously very grateful. I was surprised by his apparent wealth, and said so. "You came prepared, John. This must have been planned pretty carefully."

"Yes it was sir although it has been far more difficult than I had envisioned. And we ain't there yet. We need horses. I'm tired of that damn boat ain't you?"

Upon overhearing Surratt's diatribe Mr. Mitchin offered as to how he would be glad to take us to a friend's farm in Burgess Store, Virginia, where we could purchase horses and possibly a buggy. We accepted the offer immediately bought a few staples and told Mr. Mitchin he could have the boat. We said we called it the "Mayflower Two".

Mr. Surratt paid Thomas Jenkins in gold coins and got a lecture on how to reach the port village of Weems, Virginia, where we could cross the Rappahannock River to Middlesex County. We both thanked Jenkins and Mitchin for their help and went on our way. Thomas Jenkins who acted much the same as his friend Mitchin when we met, said that, according to the newspapers, the people up North were angry beyond belief, that nothing like this had ever happened to any Head of State anywhere, and that the South would pay dearly for their audacity. He wanted to know what would come of it and if I had agreed to be kidnapped. That puzzled me until he next said, "You seem so quiet and content Mr. Lincoln like you might enjoy being a victim. Do you want to go back? Back North, that is?"

"Yes of course I want to go back Mr. Jenkins. It is very important that we preserve the Union and bring this awful war to an end." He didn't say a word but I knew from the expression on his face that he didn't disagree.

It was a long uneventful ride bouncing about on an old buggy with iron rims on a dirt trail with plenty of holes and stones blocking the way, but we got to cross the Rappahannock River before it was too late at night to see anything, and slept in a real bed at a farmhouse near Locust Hill. This time, there was no ostensible recognition which was just as well I suppose for, once again, I was too exhausted to play the role of contented kidnappee.

WEDNESDAY, APRIL 6, 1864

Mrs. Beth Snee the widow who ran the small farm, fed us a delicious breakfast of ham and eggs and homemade bread and butter with strawberry jam. She told Mr. Surratt it would be much easier to reach Petersburg by going west toward Richmond, then turning south, than by way of Gloucester Point and Hampton. So despite Booth's previous arrangements for us to meet up with someone in Hampton we took Widow Snee's advice.

The horses having been fed and watered we set out for Richmond at 7 a.m. We would stop now and then for directions. Interestingly Surratt didn't care if people we talked to knew who I was. After all I imagine, they were all Southerners and presumably in agreement with Booth's plan to kidnap me though they probably were unaware of it beforehand. I actually began to develop a little speech to give them about the need to stop the war before Virginia could suffer any further. I told them it was hopeless and too many gallant men and boys on both sides would die or endure a lifetime of misery and suffering from near fatal injuries; that we were all Americans and should stand for one nation, indivisible.

Mr. Surratt listened as I spoke these words and never once objected or said anything to contradict what I had been preaching. Almost felt like I was campaigning again which of course I was except that I wasn't on their ballot.

We stopped for the night at a little crossroads called Adkins Store, Virginia, another post office, only 25 miles from our final destination. We arrived in late afternoon still in time to observe a great deal of activity among the citizenry. Barricades consisting of trees mostly which they were still cutting when we arrived were being built as fortifications for Confederate soldiers expected to defend against General Grant and our army. We found a farmhouse and were ushered in by the lady of the house. Although she did not notice me or recognize me, her son did.

This boy, a handsome youth about 18 or 19 had only one leg among other wounds which I could not see. He immediately waved a crutch at me as if it were a sword, and shouted profanities which I care not to repeat. "You murderous monster" he invoked, "You killed my father and brother at Gettysburg. I think you and your damn Yankees should be scalded in boiling oil and stripped of your miserable skin. I know who you are and hate you for what you have done to us. Why can't you let us go our own way? Do you have to attack us for wanting to live our way? All we want is liberty. Your way is not and never will be our way." "Mother" he said suddenly, "bring me my gun. I'm going to kill this nigger lover."

A few minutes after Stanton received the telegram about Lincoln's watch and Mr. Crudge he walked next door to the Executive Mansion to see Mrs. Lincoln. Mary Todd Lincoln was still in seclusion but agreed to see him. He told her of finding the watch on the body of Mr. Crudge.

"Will was a friend and our favorite driver" she said weeping and rubbing her eyes. "He was a fine man but I have no idea how he got my husband's watch. Do you think Mr. Lincoln gave it to him?"

Not knowing how much he should tell her Stanton let the question pass with a simple "perhaps". He assured her that to the best of his knowledge the President was safe and that the government was doing all it possibly could to get him home, whereupon he left for a meeting with people in the Navy Department. He didn't know who to see by name, but when he inquired several men began to talk about their knowledge of the Chesapeake Bay and Potomac River. Many of them had spent several years on those waters and knew what you could expect at different seasons of the year.

After describing the size and shape of a typical flat bottomed sailboat with no sail, they all agreed it would be extremely hazardous for three adult men to control a boat like that in the bay and virtually impossible for them to cross the Potomac.

"Can't be done" some men said. "And if they tried crossing when you said those boys last saw them they are all dead now. Drowned I'd say. There was a real bad storm passed through that region that same night. So I would say they are either dead or still in Maryland 'cause nobody could make that crossing in those conditions."

"If they are still alive one man added I would say they are way out on the bay by now, or out in the Atlantic Ocean and might as well be dead. If they managed to stay afloat I don't think they could reach land on the other side of the river. They would be swept out to Tangier Island or way down around Cape Charles."

Stanton thanked them for their help and went upstairs to see Gideon Welles, Secretary of the Navy. "You got anything I haven't heard about yet?" "Well, no sir. Not yet. But, we have succeeded in landing four teams of your spies on the Virginia side of the Potomac at Aquia Landing, Cole's Point, Lewisetta and Reedville. I suppose it will be a while before we hear from any of them but I'll be certain to keep you informed if and when we do."

"If?"

"Well keep in mind Mr. Stanton, these men are now spies and will face a Confederate firing squad if captured. They don't have much chance of ever returning in my judgment. I know what we would do if we caught any Confederate spies. Isn't that true?"

"Yes I'm afraid it is. But, you have to do things that you may not want to do sometimes. And in this case we have to do it. The fate of the nation may rest upon what these spies, God I hate that word, what they're able to do. I wish them well."

Stanton told Welles about the telegram from General Morris in Baltimore and of the boys having seen three men in a boat near Lookout Point.

"That's very interesting Mr. Stanton. One of our landing parties, in Reedville I do believe, spoke of a boat which they were told was especially seaworthy. It was a sort of joke there because it was named Mayflower. Two men had arrived on it a few hours before our men were put ashore."

Stanton stared at Welles angrily, "Why didn't you tell me this before damn it. This could be the break we need. Where is Reedville? Show me on your map."

"How could I have connected that boat with Lincoln's kidnapping Mr. Stanton? You hadn't told me anything about a boat. How could I have connected what I just told you with anything? I believe you owe me an apology sir. I am not guilty of withholding information!"

"And I do apologize Welles. You are correct. I truly regret having offended you in this way. Please forgive my rush to judgment. Now show me Reedville."

Welles stuck out his hand and Stanton shook it. "You are a real gentleman, Mr. Stanton. I know how much you love the President, and truly admire how hard you are trying to save him. I shall order the captain of the ship that landed our boys to find the Mayflower and bring it here as soon as possible."

Stanton smiled approval and spoke as he looked at the map and the tiny spot called Reedville. "If one of those two men was the President, which we must prove beyond any doubt, then we will know he is alive and we are hot on the trail. You have done an excellent job Mr. Secretary and I certainly appreciate it."

"Stay where you are, woman!" Surratt shouted loudly in instant response to the young amputee. "No guns or I shall be forced to shoot you both. We are going to take leave of your home and wish you no ill will if you allow us to depart peacefully. Is that agreeable to you all?"

"Get out, go, get out before I call for help and we lynch you both." He paused for only a moment then screamed at the top of his voice "You killed them. My father, my brother. I loved them and you killed them both. Please get out. I can't abide this." Then, he fell to the floor in a fetal position crying, inconsolably.

We left the house immediately, and Adkins Store. I never learned the name of the young soldier who threatened my life, nor his mother, but it was a lesson in how much sorrow war brings to people on both sides. I knew I did not kill his father or brother, in that I did not pull the trigger on the guns per se, but I knew they would both still be alive but for me. Interesting how we manage to live with ourselves.

Perhaps because of what happened at Adkins Store I have no memory of where we spent the night. Probably in the buggy, stretched out on a moonless night, happy to still be alive and all together. My memory of that night is gone.

THURSDAY, APRIL 7, 1864

Somehow, we managed to cross the James River from Wilcox's Landing to Windmill Point, and set out for the village of Prince George on our way to Petersburg.

When an old Negro holding the reins of a mule recognized me as we crossed the James, Mr. Samuel, the man who owned the ferry boat, began cursing and mumbling and muttering oaths of revenge and retaliation. Mr. Surratt stepped near me as Samuel continued his verbal abuse of Yankees Negras and me. His son, a lad of 14 or 15 put his arm around his father as if fearing I was going to attack him. I tried to smile and say nothing to fear the boy. I was not there of my own accord but decided not to say anything, just look away.

We began to notice a never ending number of wounded Confederate soldiers still in dirty, tattered uniforms of one kind or another, many helping in various ways to dig trenches and build barricades in anticipation of a battle to save the city. I knew General Grant was headed this way but I did not know where his front lines were at the moment. John said we probably should have traveled at night but it was too late now. He was as concerned as I was of the likelihood of violence if any soldiers knew I was in their midst. "You better bend down, Mr. Lincoln, I believe there is less chance they will know you if you can lower yourself until we get there." I drew my black jacket over my head and followed John's advice.

Perhaps it would have helped if one of us, or both of us, were in Southern blood stained and rumpled uniforms as dirty and torn as they were, but I would sooner die then pose as a Rebel soldier. John said he was to deliver me to a private home near the Appomattox River in the city of Petersburg, and that we were nearly there.

"I can hardly believe we did it on time" he said. "You did well Mr. Surratt" I replied "but I hope you don't leave me now, not after all we have been through. You have as good an understanding of what this war has done to the people of Virginia as I do. I pray that it will be over soon although I fear the worst. Many more will suffer and die before we can begin to reconstruct."

Petersburg was crowded with refugees from Richmond and other southern towns and villages in the path of the Union Army. I could see hundreds, perhaps thousands, of Confederate soldiers in formation being readied for the battle to come.

Mr. Angus McCreed's home on Bolingbroke Street was directly across from the slave jail. Behind his home was a shed where he had some slaves making coffins, a few pieces of furniture, and embalming the dead. Mr. McCreed was a furniture maker turned undertaker.

I followed Surratt into the back building and was accosted by two men who, without a word, handcuffed me around a pole that ran from floor to ceiling. Then, they stared at me, circled me, and laughed. "And this is what the President of the United States of America looks like" one said shaking his head slowly from side to side.

I kept my composure throughout the ordeal but wanted to sit down and have a glass of water. I tried not to think about what would happen next when John reappeared and found a chair.

"I have to bring Mr. Booth back here from Richmond Mr. Lincoln so I'll be gone for a while. But Lewis and David, the two men who are here, will take good care of you. Or at least I hope they will. You are of no value to anyone dead so they will have to be careful. Until I return then, goodbye and good luck."

Not long after that Lewis and David suddenly kicked the chair out from under me, causing me to fall hard on my tail bone, and threw some water in my face. I spent the remainder of the day and night standing or kneeling in pain, without anything to eat or drink. I could neither urinate nor defecate without soiling myself and creating a disgusting problem, but I had no choice.

Lewis turned out to be Lewis Powell, also known as Lewis Payne. A six foot two inch man from Florida, Mr. Powell had been captured at Gettysburg and paroled. The son of a minister according to what I learned later on Mr. Powell was recruited by Booth in Baltimore. A near handsome man of twenty or so, black hair blue eyes dark complexion, he was also an angry mean man who seemed to hate himself as much as anyone from up north.

David Herold his partner was a quiet young man, about the same age as Powell, but of a more even disposition. I was told that Mr. Herold had been a pharmacy clerk and enjoyed hunting. He was an outdoorsman according to Mr. Surratt but was not angry or mean.

James Mitchin saw two more strangers circling his store as he returned from his trip to Burgess Store with Lincoln and Surratt, but didn't notice the departing ship on the distant horizon. This time, he quickly surmised that these two were searching for the first two and that they were going to be asking questions, a lot of questions.

"Good afternoon gentlemen. A pleasant day for a change eh?"

"It is that sir. May we assume you to be the storekeeper here?" asked the tall younger man with a slight brogue.

"You may sir. And my name is Mitchin, James Mitchin. I have lived in these parts for all of my 66 years. Who may you be?"

"I am Michael Griffin Mr. Mitchin and my associate is Robert Williams." he said, nodding slightly toward the other man. "We are detectives with the Richmond Police in search of men wanted for high crimes and misdemeanors" Griffin lied.

"Have you any knowledge of such men Mr. Mitchin? Strangers who may have passed by here, or near here, recently?" Mr. Williams inquired.

"They are wanted for mayhem and murder."

Startled by those last few words Mitchin even surprised himself by quickly asking if there was a reward being offered for either man.

The two detectives glanced at each other, "There were only two of them," Williams said, with emphasis on the word "two", "is that correct?"

"Ah that may be gentlemen" Mitchin said slowly trying to gather his thoughts and tongue. "Let me first ask if you men have any way of showing me who you are. Some identification if you will."

Both detectives immediately opened their suit jackets to reveal small silver badges and sidearms. They showed business cards with their names over Richmond Police, Richmond, Virginia.

"The reward is negotiable Mr. Mitchin depending on how much help you can give us."

"How is it paid? Who pays it? When is it paid?" Mitchin asked excitedly.

"It can be paid here and now by us Mr. Mitchin, in gold coins. But, the amount paid may vary depending on what you tell us. Do you understand?"

"I believe I do but give me an example of how much the reward would amount to."

Griffin and Williams looked at each other before Griffin answered, "It could amount to fifty dollars Mr. Mitchin."

"For what? What would I have to tell you to get a fifty dollar reward? In gold too, is that correct?"

"Yes that's correct. A gold coin worth fifty dollars. Here and now. We would reward you for telling us, leading us better said, to where the two of them are hiding."

"I don't know where they are hiding but maybe I could tell you who might know. How much would that be worth?"

"It wouldn't be worth anything if the person you are talking about don't know or won't talk" Griffin said.

"Well I don't know if that is any good. I can't speak for him but now that I think about it I believe I know as much about this as he does. Can I get both rewards?"

"Did you recognize either man Mitchin?" Williams suddenly asked.

"Yes I did," Mitchin answered slowly. "Is there a reward for that too?"

"Let's be honest Mitchin. If you will tell us all you know about these two, all you now remember, we will pay you fifty dollars in gold."

"All I know is worth more than that Mr. Griffin. Without me you got nothing. Make it one hundred dollars and I'll even take you to where you can buy a horse."

The detectives looked at each other, gritted their teeth and agreed.

"Well where is the money?" Mitchin said, walking toward the little sailboat, called 'Mayflower'.

"It all began here on Wednesday morning." Looking at the two gold coins as he spoke James Mitchin told all he knew, and then some. He guessed that Lincoln and his companion John were going to Richmond or Petersburg; that once they crossed the Rappahannock at Weems they'd be going almost due west in order to avoid any more river crossings.

"You fellers really Yankees?" Mitchin asked innocently as he drove them out to Jenkin's stables in Burgess Store. "I guess the Yanks are mad as hell at our taking your president. I know we'd be if you took ours. Mr. Lincoln looked like a fine man, a quiet but decent sort, you know. Why would he want to start a war with us? I don't understand that. We didn't do nothing. Just want to be left alone. I hope you find him soon like. Somebody will kill him down here if they find him. I think that's understandable given all the killin' that's gone on so far."

Griffin and Williams bought two horses and left without Mr. Jenkins ever having known of the gold rewards that were available.

As soon as Griffin and Williams started down the road to Weems Mr. Mitchin headed back toward Reedville. It took but a few minutes of dwelling on riches, as he fingered the gold coins in his pocket, to concoct a plan to add to his valuable collection. Believing that the detectives were carrying even more gold coins and that killing them both, without remorse, would allow him to claim credit and be acclaimed for killing two Yankee spies, Mitchin decided to follow a narrow trail that would allow him to cross the bay at Fairport, Virginia, and ambush Griffin and Williams on their way south. He always carried a heavy Colt 44 caliber revolver with him so he knew he had the means as well as the opportunity to do himself, and his state and nation, a favor. Since he would take the bodies back to Reedville for display and credit he decided not to unhitch the horses.

It was dark and late when Mitchin standing in his wagon on a curve in the road called "Halt. Stop where you are. You are under arrest!"

Griffin and Williams stopped, puzzled by the familiar voice and command.

"Mitchin? Is that you?"

"I am arresting you both in the name of the law. Throw down your guns and hold up your hands or I will shoot."

"Hold your horses Mitchin," Williams said as he and Griffin reached for their guns. They both started firing at the same time and Mitchin was silenced forever. "Not very smart" one said to the other. "That's what greed does to you when you see gold."

Having rifled Mr. Mitchin's pockets for the gold they had paid him, his revolver, and his horses and wagon, they threw his body into a gully and went on their way, two horses pulling the buggy with two horses tethered behind. It was all over in a few minutes but James Mitchin's body would lie there forever.

FRIDAY, APRIL 8, 1864

Early this morning a well dressed well groomed man about my age entered the shed where I was being kept still handcuffed, with a terrible headache, not having been able to sleep all night. Rapidly sizing up the situation I was in and the mess I had created he allowed as to how humiliated he was to find me in such a state. "My name is McCreed Mr. Lincoln. I am without words of remorse over your condition sir. I do apologize for what they have done to you. There is no excuse. My son and I who own this business were assured that you would be well cared for if we would tolerate your stay within our facilities. We were not party to Mr. Booth's plans but, in all honesty, did not object to the idea of trying to force an end to this dreadful war."

McCreed gave me a chair to sit in and said he would have this "accident" cleaned up by his employees promptly. Also, "You may expect to stay in my home out front sir. It will be far more comfortable and I intend to reprimand those who have ill treated you so."

When they entered Angus McCreed, bless him, just stood still and looking directly at Mr. Powell and Mr. Herold, saying clearly and authoritatively, "Release this gentleman now. And don't ever do this again. What you have done is demeaning and unpardonable. I can't imagine that your leader Mr. Booth, would approve of this and I certainly plan to call it to his attention. Now release him and leave us. I do not want you here again."

Neither Powell nor Herold said a word. Mr. Powell unlocked my handcuffs and, still smelling like he fell into a barrel of whiskey, quickly left with Mr. Herold trailing behind.

I thanked Mr. McCreed and was about to ask him if I could borrow some old clothes when he, anticipating my request, said, "I will have my man help you bathe, and dress you properly in one of my suits, Mr. Lincoln. Then you will come to my home and stay with us. I am sure you are tired, and hungry too, so we will be prepared whenever you are ready."

I do not recall too well all that happened to me following McCreed's rescue except that he kept his word. I ate and slept comfortably in a very nice bed and room. Tea and crackers were brought to me by a young Negro girl as soon as I awoke. She pointed to some clothes that I was to wear and giggled, at what I knew not. Having washed my hands and face, I looked about and decided to walk downstairs when at that very moment I saw John Wilkes Booth, my tormentor, coming up the stairs.

"I want to talk to you," he said, walking into my room, drawing two chairs to a small circular table near the window.

"The politicians up north have made no moves that I'm aware of to quit this damn war and withdraw. I am fully aware that you are not as familiar as I with their transgressions since you were so unceremoniously removed from your capital last week, so I must tell you how we plan to proceed in view of their recalcitrance. Do you understand what I am saying?"

"I do so far" I said, nodding once slowly.

"Would you end the war upon your return to Washington were we to release you from captivity today?"

"No."

"Do you believe your Vice President will end the war if you do not return?"

"I have no desire to discuss that with you or anyone else considering the situation I find myself in. Does that answer your question?"

"I know that you were a prosperous attorney before becoming President, Mr. Lincoln, so I believe it reasonable to talk about this situation, as you put it, and how you would suggest we go about convincing you or your compatriots that this war must end promptly."

"As I have said Mr. Booth I do not intend to talk with you or anyone else about this matter." Booth reached for some papers in his coat pocket as I spoke, then spread them out on the table for me to inspect. Four identical letters to Vice President Hamlin, Secretary Stanton, and the leaders of the House and Senate. Each letter as you know now argued for an immediate end to all Union military activity, withdrawal of same from Confederate States, and an Act of Congress recognizing the Confederacy, with room for my signature.

"And if I do not sign them?" I asked, rhetorically.

"You'll wish you had. Remember your wife and sons are not beyond our reach. While I hate to think they would have to pay for your stubborn idiocy, I will do all I can to avoid excessive cruelty in ending their lives. I want you to mull that over, Mr. Lincoln and decide by this afternoon. Keep in mind while you meditate that my associates and I will do anything, absolutely anything, to end this war on our terms. So think not of any alternatives or escape. You are our prisoner. And we can and will do what we want with you McCreed and other mental and moral morons notwithstanding."

Thunderstruck, I stared out the window for several minutes without once moving or blinking my eyes. It was impossible to contemplate. Had everything I ever had, my family, Mary, Bob, Tad, everything I cherished beyond life itself, come down to a signature? But a signature that would, duress or no, negate or nullify everything I had stood for, fought for. God, what a world I thought. That the minds of men could devise such awful choices. I seriously thought of taking my own life, to escape the reality of consequences, no matter the decision. It was while I sat, transfixed, that John Surratt entered the room.

Stanton's spies, Michael Griffin and Robert Williams, got to cross the Rappahannock at Weems but it took time to question everyone they thought could give them the information they needed. Before long, they knew they had to have more and better identification than simple calling cards marked "Richmond Police". When they told people they were on President Jefferson Davis' staff they received instant respect and cooperation. But they needed a letter to authenticate their assertions and couldn't think of a way to forge such a letter.

Two people in Weems told the detectives that they had seen two strangers in old suits crossing over to Locust Hill late last Wednesday. "One of the men was quite tall with a thick black beard, looked sort of like President Lincoln, come to think of it. Is that who you're looking for?"

Williams shook his head slowly from side to side, smiled and kept on.

Stopping at the first farmhouse on their way to Locust Hill they encountered Mrs. Snee. While she prepared a supper for them, their small talk and good humored banter about traveling turned into a conversation about Mr. Lincoln's travails.

"I wonder if the poor man is all right," she said. "He didn't look too well you know."

"Where did you see him ma'am?" Griffin asked with a little emphasis on "you".

"Well, he was here just a few days ago. He and another man, John was his name I believe. They stayed overnight and had a big breakfast last Thursday morning. I even made some sandwiches for them to eat on their way."

"Did they say where they were going Mrs. Snee?"

Somehow the formality of that question got Beth Snee to thinking.

"Are you gentlemen friends of Mr. Lincoln?"

"We don't know him personally ma'am, but we are trying to find him to be sure he is all right. Mr. Williams here, and I, are with the Richmond Police, who have been asked by President Davis to be sure Lincoln is safe. He has been kidnapped, you know. Did John say where they were going?"

"Well I'm not sure sir." she answered warily.

Sensing a break in the case Griffin reached for his wallet and asked Mrs. Snee how much they would owe her for bed and eats. While she calculated the total he pulled out his identification and a gold coin, laying them both on the kitchen table.

"We must know ma'am. It may mean life or death for Mr. Lincoln."

She didn't hesitate to pick up the coin and tell them that John and Mr. Lincoln were going to Petersburg, which is best reached by heading west toward Richmond. "Well, you sure know that" she added smartly, "Didn't you say you were from Richmond?"

"That's right ma'am."

Early the next morning, Saturday, they set out on the same road President Lincoln and Surratt had traversed two days before. Upon reaching the small town of West Point, Virginia, at the head waters of the York River Griffin said "I have an idea, Robert" and jumped to the ground in front of a small print shop. "Follow me."

They entered the shop and after introducing themselves told the proprietor Leroy Stevens that they were on a secret mission, and that Stevens would be well paid in gold if he could help them, but could not be told what the secret mission was - only that the Richmond Police wanted some printing done by someone outside the city.

Mr. Stevens showed them how to set different kinds of type, gave them some blank stationery, and left them alone to experiment and finally produce four official looking letters in proper envelopes:

> Confederate States of America
> Office of the President
> Jefferson Davis
> Richman, Virginia
> April 8, 1864
>
> This letter is to introduce the bearer, Mr. Michael Griffin, who holds the rank of Colonel in the Army

of Northern Virginia, C. S. A., and is a key member of my staff.

Please give Colonel Griffin your full cooperation in whatever he asks. He is on a secret mission which he is under oath and orders not to reveal to anyone, on pain of death. Colonel Griffin reports to me exclusively. His is on a mission of vital concern to the Confederacy and our freedom to live as we choose.

Respectfully, your humble servant,
Jefferson Davis
President

General Robert B. Lee
Commander
Army of Northern Virginia
Confederate States of America
April 8, 1864

ORDERS

Colonel Michael Griffin, C. S. A., the bearer of this order is to be provided with whatever financial and material assistance he requires in his judgment in order to complete a secret mission known only to him and the President of the Confederate States of America.

As a member of President Jefferson Davis' military staff, Colonel Griffin reports to the President exclusively.

You are therefore ordered to cooperate with Colonel Griffin to the fullest extent possible, including immediate and safe passage through our lines and unmonitored use of our telegraph systems.

By order of
Signed:
General Robert B. Lee

After changing the name to Robert Williams and printing a few extra copies, they paid the printer, Stevens, one hundred dollars in two gold coins, signed the documents and left, but forgot to decompose the type thus allowing Stevens to run copies for his inspection.

Continuing on toward Richmond newly commissioned Colonels Griffin and Williams laughed at their audacity and decided to get appropriate uniforms and insignia as soon as possible. One more night sleeping in their wagon and they would be safely sheltered in a first class Petersburg hotel. They could have taken the Richmond and York Railroad to Richmond, and then to Petersburg, but were too excited when they left the printers to inquire about trains.

Angry that he had fallen for a fraudulent scheme upon reading what his two customers had produced, Leroy Stevens knew that he had a patriotic if not moral, obligation to report what had happened and give the proper officials, notably Mr. Davis himself, copies of the letters and orders so that justice might be done. He knew those two men were up to no good, that they might even be Yankee spies. He decided to close his shop and go to Richmond immediately.

Having written a brief but bitter letter to Vice President Hannibal Hamlin, Major General George McClellan went about visiting the editors and publishers of newspapers in Washington. "I believe the office of President of the United States should be declared vacant if the President, no matter who he may be, and for whatever reason, cannot discharge his duties as prescribed by The Constitution."

McClellan was adamant that some action be taken by the Vice President to declare himself President, now. The vacancy of eight days, and uncertainty as to how many more days the country would be left without a leader was unacceptable. Not knowing if Mr.

Lincoln would ever return, McClellan, the likely candidate of the National Democrat Party to challenge Lincoln in the November 1864 general election, felt he was on strong ground in speaking out now in a not very well disguised effort to kill any chance of losing the election in the fall. If Lincoln could be removed from office in this way, McClellan was confident that he could not get back on the ballot as the Republican candidate. People were fed up with the war and wanted someone to end it. McClellan would, and everyone knew it. The U. S. Senate had passed a joint resolution 38-6 abolishing slavery and approving the 13th Amendment to the Constitution. In the House, Ohio Democrat Alexander H. Long called for recognition of Confederate Independence: "I am reluctantly and despondingly forced to conclude that the Union is lost, never to be restored."

SATURDAY, APRIL 9, 1864

There wasn't much rest for anyone in war weary Virginia on any day any more.

I had a long discussion with Mr. Surratt in the privacy of my room at McCreed's, and meditated for a while before taking a much needed nap.

Mr. Surratt told me that Booth would no doubt send the letters after forging my signature, and that they would be delivered by specially selected underground couriers to friends in the capital who would make sure they would get to the addressees. Not to worry however Surratt advised. "The letters are not going to do the job" he said "because they know up North you are being held against your will."

On Saturday afternoon Booth returned to McCreed's with Horace Shoemaker, the sole proprietor of a popular photography studio. Business had been good since the beginning of the war what with so many soldiers wanting a nice daguerreotype portrait of themselves in uniform as a keepsake gift for their girlfriend, wife, or mother.

"I want four photographs of us, Lincoln and I together, and four of Lincoln alone with his left hand in bandages."

"I don't believe I understand Mr. Booth. What is the purpose of the second photograph?"

"The purpose is, Mr. Shoemaker, to show that we mean business. If those warmongers in Washington understand that we mean to take Lincoln apart, piece by piece, until they relent, and withdraw from the Southern States of America then the daguerreotypes and others like it will have been worth the effort. Don't you agree?"

"I'm not sure I agree with that Mr. Booth. I don't recall ever being asked to take a picture of that kind and certainly not of a man like Abraham Lincoln. That picture, if it were ever circulated, would cause a lot of people to become angry, really angry, maybe even at me."

"Not you Shoemaker, me. But that's not for you to worry. Their anger would be directed at the cause of all this, the war! People would, upon seeing that photograph and the dead hand which will also appear demand that the Vice President and U. S. Congress bring an end to atrocities, wherever thay may occur. But, take my word as a guarantee, Mr. Shoemaker, this war will end and the South will triumph!" John Wilkes Booth acted as if he were on a stage shouting the last few words of a soliloquy.

"Whose dead hand Mr. Booth? My God do you intend to amputate Mr. Lincoln's hand? If so, I will have nothing to do with this abomination, sir. I have a reputation to protect Mr. Booth, and I'll not sacrifice it for a devilish scheme such as this no matter how you attempt to justify it. You better get another photographer. I want no part of this." Lincoln overheard some of this loud talk and wondered. Standing stock-still, his big black mustache actually quivering, Booth ordered Horace Shoemaker to get out, that he, John Wilkes Booth, would find a man with the courage and patriotism needed now. Booth left McCreed's to find Powell and Herold. He knew he could count on them.

Although Jefferson Davis was not in his office when Leroy Stevens arrived, Major Forrest Busby, C.S.A., his military aide-de-camp listened carefully to what Stevens had to say, then read the letter and orders purporting to be those of Davis and Lee. Alarmed at what he heard and read and trusting Mr. Stevens implicitly, Major Busby hurried downstairs to the provost marshal's office where he told Steven's story, produced the evidence and asked, on behalf of President Davis, that the two would-be colonels be found immediately. Three provost sergeants were ordered to find and imprison or shoot them as spies.

After purchasing new uniforms that were tailored to fit perfectly, for after all they had rank and gold to match, Colonels Griffin and Williams returned to their rooms at the Virginia Hotel where they had registered earlier in the afternoon. A large tavern next door to the hotel had caught their eye as they left their horses and buggy with the Negro youngster who promised to care for them and the wagon in a stable behind the hotel. When Griffin threw him a gold coin, the boy's eyes nearly popped out.

Swaggering up to the bar with swagger stick in hand and Williams trailing quietly close behind, 'Colonel' Griffin, C.S.A., called for a bottle of the best bourbon whiskey in the house. "One for 'Colonel' Williams too" Griffin demanded and paid in gold. After a few drinks, Colonel Griffin became quite talkative.

"I want you to know sir" he said to the bartender, and to others who were also standing at the beautiful mahogany bar, complete with a brass rail, "I want you to know that we are drawing close to our man, that our mission, secret as it is, is almost over, and we can return to the front lines and resume our battle against those bumbling bastards of Birmingham."

Griffin and Williams were each about one third of the way through their bourbon when two pretty girls asked if they would join them for a little celebration of Miss Lola's birthday. Colonels Griffin and Williams readily assented, ordered two bottles of the best champagne, and joined the girls at a table toward the rear of the tavern.

After some quick introductions Miss Lola Leonard and Miss Trudy Jackson told the Confederate officers how much they admired their courage and bravery, that they were the two best looking men they had ever seen, that their uniforms and high rank entitled them to anything, anything they wanted, upstairs or downstairs.

As Lola and Trudy carefully poured their cheap champagne into a pot behind the table, and Griffin and Williams continued celebrating with bourbon, a few men at the bar began discussing the unbecoming condition of their fellow bar patrons, and especially the copies of Mr. Davis' letter and Robert E. Lee's orders, which Colonel Griffin had given the barkeeper to inspect.

"This doesn't look right Will" one man said, "Both of these are dated the same, April 8, and on the same kind of paper. And look here, Richmond is spelled wrong, and wait, you ever hear of Robert B. Lee? 'B' as in boy. Who ever heard of Robert B. Lee?"

"And there is information missing," said another. "Military orders are always numbered, and Lee's don't have no numbers. How do you explain that?"

"I don't explain it. Let's join their party over there and ask them. I'll be damned but they don't look like colonels are supposed to look. Let's go."

"Would you gentlemen mind if we joined your party for a bit? We're pretty proud of our soldiers down here in Pete, and want you to know we stand with you all the way" said one man.

"That's behind you," another said with what passed as wit, "That's behind you but still with you."

"Did you say you fought in Birmingham?" another asked quickly.

Griffin paused, took another long drink and said, "We fought everywhere Lee went."

"It must have been awful" Will remarked. "That Battle of Birmingham especially."

"Yes, lost a lot of men," Williams added.

"Where the hell was that Birmingham battle fought?" a third man said, "Near Montgomery?"

"Ayuh," Griffin said, "Near Montgomery."

"Florida?"

"Ayuh."

"What do we do now?" one of the locals said to another as they slowly backed away toward the bar talking privately about what they had seen and heard.

"I think we just got to get them drunk, I mean real drunk, and lock 'em up 'till we can get the sheriff or the army in here to take over.

I don't know what to do even though I'm personally convinced these two are imposters. They are not who they say they are." Quietly the others agreed and let Griffin and Williams continue drinking.

"They're stayin' at the Virginia, so why don't we let the girls here take 'em home and lock 'em up till we get somebody?"

"That makes sense. Hell get them really loaded. Meantime I'm going to go look for some military police."

Drunk but happy, Colonels Griffin and Williams climbed the stairs to their adjoining rooms on the second floor, facing the street, with Miss Lola and Miss Trudy. Griffin was singing the "Battle Hymn of the Republic" loudly enough to be heard in the lobby.

Two Confederate military policemen knocked respectfully on the their doors a short time later. Only half clothed, Lola opened the door just far enough for the two men to enter forcibly. When they began asking Griffin and Williams to identify themselves, neither man could provide any information other than a bleary reference to a secret mission, a mission to find President Lincoln.

"Thase a secret, so keep it a secret," one of them said in a whiskey soaked voice. "Nobody but us know he's in town, so keep it a secret men. Nobody knows but us. And, we're gonna take him home. We have orders. You'll see. Where are those damn letters?"

The police conferred and after telling the girls to leave decided to arrest the colonels and take them to the county prison near the courthouse down by the river.

"You can't arrest us, we're officers and gentlemen. Why are you arresting us? Where did the girls go? Want to make some money? Real money. Gold. We've got gold, lots of gold. Juss let us be or, hell, juss let us be and I'll give you fifty gold dollars. Fifty real U. S. gold dollars. Fifty each, and a drink. We've got lots of drinks. Get another bottle. Get the girls back, we'll have a party. I'll pay."

Booked into the county jail as Confederate States Army prisoners, the deputy sheriff jailer gave them receipts for 240 dollars in gold coins, and two almost empty bottles of Kentucky bourbon. He took the remaining 500 dollars in gold as his finding fee.

SUNDAY, APRIL 10, 1864

Late this morning, Powell and Herold came and took me from my room to the shed out back where they did some embalming. They told me to sit and be quiet or I would be subdued, so I sat and waited for whatever was going to happen next. I noticed a large camera on a table facing me and then saw my nemesis Booth enter the shed.

David Herold got behind the big clumsy camera, under a photographer's curtain or drape, and told me to look straight ahead with my eyes open. Booth was standing directly behind me. I tried hard not to blink but the bright lights in my face forced me to squint a bit. Powell finally said it was done whereupon they seized me while still seated and wrapped my left hand in dirty blood soaked cloths. I didn't resist because it would have been pointless. They had the strength to do what they wanted with me, so I let them.

As someone moved a small table in front of me I was told to look at the table and not move. There on the table was a human hand. "Is this your definition of theater?" I asked of him. "I think your brother Edwin, would disagree. Vehemently. I just saw him a few days ago in Hamlet and

Richard III at Grover's Theater. Do not carry this outrage forward Booth. Edwin would be disgusted. Where did this hand come from? I would like to pray for the victim, to think that an unfortunate human being could be forced to become proxy to your chicanery is simply beyond redemption. This is grotesque."

Booth simply said "shut up", nodded at Powell, pointed toward the door, and I was taken back to my room. I fell into my melancholy, hoping to God that our people would see through this utterly vile attempt to influence them.

I lay abed with my eyes open and my mind skipping around trying to make some sense out of what had happened since our carriage was stopped in Silver Spring so long ago. Eleven days seemed like an eternity.

As my anxiety deepened, I tried to decide if it was my mind or my brain that was working against me. I forced myself to do numbers, though they meant nothing. How many seconds in a day? A week? 24 by 60 by 60. That's 86,400. And, in a year? No, wait, it has to be 86,400 per day times 52 for a year. How much is that? Why am I doing this? To keep from thinking.

No. No. It's 86,400 times 7 days in a week, then by 52. What is that number? I need a pencil and paper. No. No. I was talking to myself. Was I going insane? I forced myself back to multiplying in my head. Seven times 86,400 is zero, zero, carry the two, seven 6's are 42, plus 2 is 44, zero, zero, 84, carry the 4, seven 8's are 56, plus 4 is 60. It must be 604,800. I did it again, to be sure. Now, I'm rolling from side to side atop the bed in frustration. I can do it. 604,800 seconds per week by 52 weeks is? Must be something over

30 million. Ten times 600,000 is 6 million, 100 times is 60 million, and half of that is 30 million. That's close, but not enough. I would have to do it correctly, 52 not 50, and the correct number 604,800, not 600,000. By this time, my brain must have grown weary and fallen asleep, for when I woke, I didn't have the answer to that little arithmetic problem. I would try again later. I didn't feel well, in my head or my abdomen, and I didn't know why. I wondered what they were doing in Washington and if General Grant had made any progress since his arrival and early departure to take command in the field early last month. Then, I remembered my favorite poem. I had memorized it in its entirety many years ago, and recited it so often that some folks mistook me as the author. It is called 'Mortality':

Oh, why should the spirit of mortal be proud?
Like a swift-fleeting meteor, a fast-flying cloud,
A flash of the lightning, a break of the wave,
He passes from life to his rest in the grave.
The leaves of the oak and the willow shall fade,
Be scattered around, and together be laid;
And the young and the old, the low and the high,
Shall molder to dust, and together shall lie.
The infant a mother attended and loved;
The mother that infant's affection who proved;
The husband, that mother and infant who blessed;
Each, all, are away to their dwelling of rest.
The maid on whose cheek, on whose brow, in whose eye,
Shone beauty and pleasure - her triumphs are by;

And the memory of those who loved her and praised,
Are alike from the minds of the living erased.
The hand of the king that the sceptre hath borne,
The brow of the priest that the mitre hath worn,
The eye of the sage, and the heart of the brave,
Are hidden and lost in the depths of the grave.
The peasant, whose lot was to sow and to reap,
The herdsman, who climbed with his goats up the steep,
The beggar, who wandered in search of his bread,
Have faded away like the grass that we tread.
The saint, who enjoyed the communion of Heaven,
The sinner, who dared to remain unforgiving,
The wise and the foolish, the guilty and just,
Have quietly mingled their bones in the dust.
So the multitude goes – like the flower or the weed
That withers away to let others succeed;
So the multitude comes – even those we behold,
To repeat every take that has often been told.
For we are the same that our fathers have been;
We see the same sights that our fathers have seen;
We drink the same stream, we feel the same sun,
And run the same course that our fathers have run.
The thoughts we are thinking, our fathers would think;
From the death we are shrinking, our fathers would
shrink;
To the life we are clinging, they also would cling –
But it speeds from us all like a bird on the wing.
They loved – but the story we cannot unfold;
They scorned – but the heart of the haughty is cold;
They grieved – but no wail from their slumber will come;

They joyed – but the tongue of their gladness is dumb.
They died – aye, they died – we things that are now,
That walk on the turf that lies over their brow,
And make in their dwellings a transient abode,
Meet the things that they met on their pilgrimage road.
Yea, hope and despondency, pleasure and pain,
Are mingled together in sunshine and rain;
And the smile and the tear, the song and the dirge,
Still follow each other, like surge upon surge.
'Tis the wink of an eye – 'tis the draught of a breath –
From the blossom of health to the paleness of death,
From the gilded saloon to the bier and the shroud
Oh, why should the spirit of mortal be proud?

When Edwin Stanton received word from Gideon Welles that the Mayflower Two had arrived, he hurried over to the Navy Department for a close inspection. President Lincoln must have left something in or on the small boat if this was how, in fact, he arrived in Reedville, Virginia. Welles said the little store was still there, locked up, but the storekeeper was gone. No one knew where he had gone or when he'd return, but they all agreed that Lincoln had been there. There was no evidence that the boat had been used in transit, until Stanton asked that it be turned on its side. There, in letters some an inch high, was the name, barely decipherable, 'Lincoln', scratched near the bow, just below the narrow wooden passenger grip rail that framed the boat.

"Strange place to find his name" Stanton observed. "He would have had to be in the water to do this because his name is not upside down. How else could he have done it? Perhaps he was steering the boat. This rudder doesn't look like it works too well."

"That may be so but I think we can agree that Lincoln was alive when this little boat landed."

"You are right. Now we know he got to Virginia. That tells me we have to meet with Hamlin, Bates and the others today to talk about political strategy, and how to deal with the copperheads. I understand that George McClellan is trying to force Hamlin to take over the presidency permanently, which is just a clever way to get rid of the only man who can beat him in November."

"And sacrifice the Union in the process," Welles added. "How is Grant doing in Virginia?"

"It's going to be costly. He is planning to take Richmond, but Lee's not going to give up easily. He's strong enough to hold for awhile. Sherman is fighting his way down to Atlanta. Let's you and I go see Hamlin. I want to know how he feels bout McClellan's demands. The newspapers in New York and Philadelphia are playing that issue on the front page, as well as editorializing, so we have to get this under control."

The two secretaries walked into Vice President Hamlin's office. Stanton picked up one of the local papers and read aloud:

**"Major General George McClellan demands
V.P. Hamlin seize presidency. No word from
Booth on Lincoln's condition. General says V.P.
must declare top office vacant. President may be dead."**

"That is why we are here. Can you get Bates and Seward in here? We've got to have a conference."

In a few minutes William Seward, Secretary of State, and Edward Bates, the Attorney General, gathered around a highly polished conference table to hear the Secretary of War recapitulate dramatic events of the past 11 days and then ask: "Where do we go from here gentlemen? What happens next?"

"Well if I may," Mr. Bates began, "We have got something more than a political problem here. This is a constitutional problem, perhaps even a crisis. The country can't continue without a President, a Head of State. We can do it for awhile but not indefinitely. No one knows if Mr. Lincoln's coming back or when, or if he's even alive."

"He's alive" Stanton spoke out loudly.

"Well, I hope so, but that won't do us any good if he is not back here alive. You understand that. And, you know that the Constitution is silent on the subject of vacancy. Who is to decide what constitutes vacancy? The Vice President? Congress? The Supreme Court? Is a vacancy created by a kidnap such as we have here sufficient to meet the rule? What rule? Who says Lincoln won't return tomorrow? And what if the Vice President takes over permanently and signs new legislation, makes appointments, and does a thousand other things that presidents do? Are they legal? Some of them would probably be challenged in the courts. And you all know what that would mean. The cost of litigation like that in dollars alone, not to speak of the problems it would create for the litigants and the country, would be horrendous. I believe as all of you surely do that whatever we do must be iron-clad legal. Now how do you convince people like McClellan, and the Congress, and Roger Taney our Chief Justice? They may not see it as we do."

MONDAY, APRIL 11, 1864

Upon receiving a telegraph message from his Petersburg office in which a Captain Long told of the arrest and incarceration of two men, Colonel Henry Macon was elated.

> April 10, 1864
> Captain J. Long,
> Provost Marshal
> Confederate Army District
> Petersburg, Virginia
> Attention: Colonel Henry Macon,
> Provost Marshal, C.S.A.
> Army of Northern Virginia
>
> Two men named Michael Griffin and Robert Williams posing as colonels in C.S. Army of Northern Virginia in correct military uniforms and bearing a letter purportedly Signed by President Davis and orders signed by General Robert E. Lee, stating they are on a secret mission were arrested and incarcerated here last night. Both men were drunk. Their mission to locate and return President Lincoln to Washington was nearly done. On President Davis' letter, Capital City was spelled 'Richman'. On General Lee's orders, his name appeared as Robert B. Lee. Griffin and Willliams answer description of men wanted per your telegraph message to all districts Sunday April 9, regarding possible spies. Please advise.
>
> J. Long
> Captain, C.S.A.

Colonel Macon, after conferring with President Davis, organized and led a firing squad, a small contingency of eight enlisted men, to Petersburg, on Monday afternoon. He and another officer in his command, an attorney in civilian life, met Colonels Griffin and Williams in jail. No longer in uniform, and interviewed separately, each man was told he would die as a spy if he could not or would not answer questions to the satisfaction of Colonel Macon.

Q. What is your real name?
A. Michael Griffin
Q. Where were you born?
A. Ireland
Q. Where do you make your home?
A. Well here I guess. I like it here.
Q. How long have you lived here?
A. All my life I guess.
Q. What is your address here?
A. It's a farm. Out west. Someplace.
Q. Who gave you the letter from President Davis?
A. President Davis.
Q. What does he look like?
A. I don't know how to rightly answer that one sir. It was dark and I never could see too good. He looked like you. Medium height and weight. Dark hair.
Q. Who gave you the gold?
A. President Davis.
Q. Who gave you the orders from General Lee?
A. General Lee.
Q. Why did he sign his name as Robert B. Lee?
A. 'Cause that's his name.
Q. Do you think he knows that his name is Robert E. Lee?
A. Sure, I guess.
Q. Then why would he sign it Robert B., instead of Robert E.?
A. I don't know. Maybe he can't see too good.
Q. Do you know a man named Leroy Stevens?
A. No.

Q. A print shop proprietor named Leroy Stevens?

A. I don't think so.

Q. He says you set the type and printed these documents on his press, in his shop. Do you deny that?

A. Yes. He's a liar.

"No, Mr. Griffin. You are the liar. Mr. Stevens gave us copies of these documents while still unsigned and a description of you and Williams. Now why don't you tell us who you really are and why you're down here in Petersburg. If you cooperate with us we may take that into consideration. And remember we have yet to question Mr. Williams. President Davis never met you. We asked him that question and his answer was no. Your description of him is also wrong. He is a tall, thin, man. Hardly of medium stature and does not look at all like me."

"Robert E. Lee can see quite well. And while it would be easy for a Yankee to hear an E as a B, or a B as an E, it is inconceivable that General Lee would sign his own name incorrectly. You do not have much choice Mr. Griffin. We will give you some time to think this over and make your final decision but keep in mind, I can give you no guarantee that you will live even if you do talk. That may depend on what Williams tells us."

Robert Williams knew that it was all over. He didn't have to be asked any questions. As soon as Colonel Macon and Lieutenant Dix, his assistant, entered his cell he started confessing, throwing himself on the mercy of his enemies.

He told of how both he and Griffin had been requisitioned from the New York City Police Department, Detective Bureau, by Edwin Stanton, the Secretary of War, and how Stanton had personally briefed them and made arrangements with the U. S. Navy to land them in Virginia, and search for President Lincoln.

Williams said Lincoln was here now, somewhere in Petersburg, that they had picked up the trail in Reedville and followed it only a day or possibly two behind Lincoln and another man named "John" something. He said that he and Griffin would have been able to find the President simply by finding and following John Wilkes Booth, who would, unknowingly, lead them to where Lincoln was being held captive. The Davis letter and Lee's orders would have given them carte blanche in returning Lincoln to Washington.

Macon was dumbfounded at these revelations and politically astute enough to know that he should not go ahead with a firing squad execution of the spies without first briefing President Davis, who almost certainly did not know that his arch enemy was only a few miles away, somewhere in Petersburg.

Hurriedly and without saying anything to anyone, Colonel Macon and Lieutenant Dix left the jail to catch the next train to Richmond, not realizing that Captain Long could and would assume that the execution of Griffin and Williams was to take place. Why else would Colonel Macon have brought a firing squad with him from the capitol? Why would he not have ordered the execution to be postponed, or nullified if it were not to take place? Why, if the execution was not to take place now, would he have not ordered the firing squad to return to Richmond or find quarters in Petersburg?

Captain Long knew his prisoners were spies. Williams had even confessed to a jail guard this morning.

Long ordered the provo sergeant in charge of the detail to load their rifles, march the prisoners from their cells to a small courtyard adjacent to the jail, tie them to posts and blindfold them, if they wished. He, Captain Long, would give the signal to fire, and he said he expected them to aim at each man's heart; that of the eight bullets to be used, two were blank cartridges, so no one would ever know which rifles actually killed the enemy spies.

"When my arm drops, fire." Long said as the squad took their places. A few minutes later, Captain Long personally shot Michael Griffin and Robert Williams in the head with his pistol, the time honored coup de grace, even though both men were already dead.

After giving each man in the squad a glass of whiskey and ordering them to return to Richmond, Captain Long sat down and wrote a short message to be telegraphed to Colonel Macon:

> Our enemies' spies Griffin and Williams were executed by your firing squad at 4:05 p.m. today.
> J. Long
> Captain C.S.A.
> April 11, 1864

Fortunately, for what was left of Colonel Macon's military career in the Rebel Army, he saw the telegram before Jefferson Davis asked him what happened to those two spies he caught in Petersburg.

"We shot them Mr. President," he said, showing Davis the telegraph message from Captain Long. "I went down there you know and questioned them both. Guilty. Both of them. No doubt about it."

"Thank you, Colonel. I'll see that that is made a part of your record. You did a fine job."

TUESDAY, APRIL 12, 1864

When Angus McCreed began to notice several small clusters of men and women gathering outside his home, pointing at both the front and back buildings, he became suspicious and nervous. Endless talk about the Dahlgren-Kilpatrick raid in late February and early March had reached a boiling point throughout Virginia, but especially in Richmond and Petersburg. People were very angry about what happened, and what would have happened had the raid been successful. Their fury was directed at President Lincoln for having authorized it and what was supposed to follow. According to papers supposedly found on Colonel Dahlgren's body, where he was ambushed in King and Queen County on March 2, 1864, the President of the Confederate States of America, Jefferson Davis and his cabinet were to be killed, and the city of Richmond burned to the ground.

Although there were a few who questioned the validity of the papers found the vast majority of people were convinced that Lincoln, a known admirer of Colonel Dahlgren's father Admiral John A. Dahlgren, instigated the attack and ordered the killing and destruction that was to follow.

The raid itself was conceived by Brigadier General Judson Kilpatrick as a way to set free the Union soldiers being held captive at the notorious Libby Prison in Richmond. Some of the prisoners had escaped and described conditions at the prison as abominable. People in the north were astounded by what they heard and called for action to free the prisoners.

And, so it was that 4500 Union troops, led by Kilpatrick, started out toward Richmond on February 28. Colonel Dahlgren leading about 500 men headed west and south from above Richmond while Kilpatrick reached Richmond on the north side.

General Kilpatrick soon realized that it was a hopeless venture and began his escape by leading his forces down the peninsula to the safety of Fortress Monroe.

Dahlgren was not as fortunate. He and his men were ambushed by General Custis Lee while trying to catch up with Kilpatrick's retreat.

So infuriated by what they heard and thought to be true Virginians, soldiers and civilians alike, pledged renewed vigor and vengeance against the Yankee Army and Abraham Lincoln in particular.

He was a pariah who would be killed on sight, as he would have had Jefferson Davis killed.

Taking a cigar from his humidor on the big table in the front room, Angus McCreed lit up and watched as the crowd grew larger. He suspected that people in Peterburg had somehow learned that President Lincoln was being held here, in his home. But, how could that have happened? Surely no one in his business would have leaked that news. Nor his son. But Booth? That didn't make any sense. Booth so far had made an effort to keep Lincoln's presence here a closely guarded secret. Was there some other reason growing numbers of people were gathering out front? He decided to go upstairs and talk with the President. Lincoln was sleeping again. McCreed was about to waken him when John Surratt came in the room.

"Let him sleep Mr. McCreed. He has not been feeling well, in the brain you know and the belly. I ain't sure what's wrong, but somtin is. He says he dreams a lot. And they ain't good dreams."

"Have you seen that crowd outside?"

"I've seen them, and heard them."

"What do they want?"

"They seem to think, maybe they know, that we're holding President Lincoln. But I don't know if that is good or bad. I can't tell if they want him to make a speech, or hang him."

"Or both."

"What do you think we ought to do?"

"Well he's your prisoner, John. It's up to you. Do you deny he's here? Or hide him? Or get him out of here?"

"Well he is my prisoner Mr. McCreed but this is your home and business, and if those people…."

"I know what you're saying, if they are angry I have a problem."

"We'll both have a problem. To deny it is to invite even more trouble. They just might decide to hang you - and me - if they get real angry and think we're protecting him."

"And trying to hide him would not work. There is no place here where we could hide him."

"Then we better move him. Right away because the bigger that mob gets the harder it's going to be."

"I would wager there are a thousand people out there already" McCreed observed squinting at the ever increasing number out front but standing back from the lace curtains on the windows. He chewed frantically on the cigar. "How you going to do it John?"

"I don't know. Ain't never dealt with a mob before. Maybe they ain't angry."

Then a rock broke one of the front windows and some men began to yell.

"What are they saying John? I can't make it out."

"They're chanting different…sounds mostly like "lynch Lincoln, lynch Lincoln, lynch, lynch, lynch. This is a lynch mob Mr. McCreed. And it ain't going to be no fun, but I got an idear."

"What are you going to do?"

"Let me ask you first if we do get him out of here where can we take him? Where is a good safe place near here? Walking distance?"

"Let me think. I don't know of anybody. Let me think."

"Who was that photographer that Booth brought in a few days ago?"

"You must be talking about Shoemaker. Horace Shoemaker. I saw Booth come in past my office. Good man. He has a studio not far from here."

"Walking distance?"

"Why yes but what makes you think he would offer his premises as a refuge?"

"That comes later Mr. McCreed. Right now I've got to plan some kind of escape route for all of us."

"How you going to do it?"

"Well the first I got to do is get him out of bed and tell him what's going on. Then I am gonna have to get him to agree with my plan. And he may not want to do it. While I'm doing that I want you to get some soap and a razor. We will have to help him cut off his beard."

"What does his beard have to do with this?"

"Well Angus, it's the only way I can think of getting out of here. Can't walk him out or take him out in a wagon. But if we cut off his beard and tell him to hold onto his belt so as to make him shorter, and dress in plain clothes like those folks out there, maybe we can mix with them when they get in here. It will be dark and confusing. We would have a chance to become part of the crowd."

"I wish Booth was here" McCreed sighed, "This was his idea. He could talk to them and calm them down."

Several more rocks started to hit the house and windows.

"He is up in Richmond making speeches."

"I will go get Rufus to cut off the beard."

"Better not Angus. They have probably surrounded the house by now and you would be caught, and hung."

"Hung? You think they would do that to me? These people are my neighbors, my friends. Why would they hang me?"

"'Cause a mob don't think, Angus. All they want is blood, the blood of anybody who stands in their way."

"Well, I don't believe that John. I'll take your word for it now but I have known these people all my life, lived among them, and they know me. No sir they would never hang me."

John gently awakened me. He told me what was happening and asked if I understood the danger we were in.

"I believe I do but it is me they want, not you or Mr. McCreed. Why don't you let me handle this and keep my beard, which I've come to like."

"No sir we've come this far and safely and I'm not going to give you up that easily, especially to a mob."

After explaining his plan and telling me that he expected cooperation because the lives of other people in the house may depend upon it, I said nothing for several minutes.

"I know you are trying to help me John and help the others. I am sorry that my personage has brought this down on you so if you want to go ahead with your plan I will help and do whatever you say. Is that enough?" Angus McCreed's eyes were watering slightly as he handed me a warm wet towel and a bar of soap. "Rufus will be here in a moment. I found him and the others downstairs. Everyone is out of the back shed. Fortunately my son is out of town on business. Rufus does all the cosmetic work on our clientele, including hair of course, so let him remove the beard, and cut your hair some."

The chanting and Rebel yells had increased in volume and intensity as rocks kept belting the house. It was growing dark.

"I think we'll wait downstairs somewhere" John said. "Wait until they break into the house, and fill the room. The big room. While they're doing that we can slip into the crowd and start backing out the door. You should not do any screaming or yelling yourself. Let me do that. I'll try to cover your face as best I can. You keep down and don't look up at anybody, including me. With your beard gone and hair cut and eyebrows trimmed" he said, looking at me from different angles "we might just get out of here alive."

Yelling and screaming for vengeance the mob moved closer and closer, hurling stones and other objects at the house, but stopped suddenly, as the front door opened and someone appeared carrying a torch. He raised his arm and spoke.

"I am Angus McCreed. You know me and my family. I know you, my friends and neighbors. You have always trusted me so I beg you to trust me now." The crowd was getting restless.

"Give us Lincoln Angus," a man shouted in the nearby moonless night. "We're going to lynch Lincoln Angus, now get him," another yelled out. McCreed knew he was losing control.

"Trust me" he shouted. "Lincoln is not here." But the mob didn't agree. "Give us Lincoln" several cried out in unison, then began to chant "lynch Lincoln, lynch Lincoln," as they moved ever closer to seize McCreed. Several hundred people began to move toward the house, while others threw a rope around a low branch of the old oak tree in the front yard. The burning torch caught the lace curtains in the broken windows and as the mob filled the front room, so did the fire. A very frightened man Angus McCreed could be seen in the light of that fire being hung from the old tree in the front of his home as the mob kept screaming, "We want Lincoln!" Twenty-two people died in the house that night, from suffocation, smoke inhalation and stampede. Rufus, and another black man were hung next to their master, but John Surratt, Powell, Atzerodt and I escaped, just as John had planned.

No one knew Angus McCreed would do what he did but John wasn't surprised. "Poor guy tried to save us" he said. "He didn't understand how much the people have suffered and hate this war. He just managed the place. Rufus and his son did all the embalming, but never discussed it with the old man. So he didn't know how bad it is. Now ain't that somtin? Tells me we got to find Booth and get him to do somtin soon, or someday we're all gonna lose our luck."

WEDNESDAY, APRIL 13, 1864

Despite their defeat for governor in Ohio and Pennsylvania, two still influential Democrat politicians, Copperhead Clement

Vallandigham of Ohio, and Judge George Woodward of Pennsylvania, were able to prevail upon a mutual friend in the U. S. Congress to introduce a bill to compel the Vice President of the United States to declare the Office of President permanently vacant, and thus assume all of the duties and responsibilities of that office after being properly sworn in, if the President is physically absent or unable to perform his duties under the constitution, no matter the reason for a period of 30 consecutive days.

Archer W. Owens a second term member of the U. S. House of Representatives from George McClellan's home district in New Jersey, filed the bill with the House clerk the day after Edwin Stanton met, unofficially, with other members of President Lincoln's cabinet, on Sunday, April 10.

That same day, newspapers all over the country, especially in Chicago, New York, Philadelphia and Washington, featured the move on their front pages:

Congress to debate bill to declare Lincoln's office vacant.
President may have only 30 days to appear.
Only 19 days left!

Archer Owen's interviews with the press revealed the influence that pro-slavery Vallandigham and Woodward had on him, but the New York Herald Reporter was able to work Major General McClellan, Lincoln's most likely opponent in the coming elections of 1864, into the story.

"The major benefactor should this resolution pass," his story said, "is of course Major General George B. McClellan, who has made it clear to one and all that he would immediately stop the war and bring our lads home, if elected."

Lars F. (Ace) Sohlgren, the reporter, said that both Vallandigham and Woodward were old family friends of the McClellan's and that Owens was only trying to do everyone a favor. Owens bill has been assigned to the House Judiciary Committee and will probably be acted upon with great haste. "Time now is of the essence," Congressman Owens noted. "I expect my bill will attract some who will disagree, and may want to testify before the committee, but we cannot allow this to continue indefinitely. True, Mr. Lincoln was legally elected to the office in 1860, and true, it is no fault of his, that we know of now, that he was abducted on March 31, this year, but we must think of the country as a whole. We are a nation without a Head of State. And, such a nation, absent a leader who has clear legal grounds for whatever action is needed, whenever, is a nation that is doomed to fail. The issue here is neither slavery nor union. It is simply put survival. Lincoln or anyone else in his position and I for one deeply sympathize with his wife and children, is expendable. The nation is greater than the parts thereof. Survive we must, and so my bill says after 30 days, which is a long time when a protracted war continues without end, we must act!"

Edwin Stanton, as soon as he heard of Owen's bill, went over to see Vice President Hamlin. "I don't know how far McClellan will get with this, but I think we've got to stop it before the public starts to pressure their representatives to vote favorably. Do you believe we can stop it from being introduced in the Senate?"

"It's too late. It was filed this morning by two senators, co-sponsors."

"Who? Who would do that?"

"It's a pretty clever move actually. Douglas and Johnson filed the same bill Archer Owens filed over in the House. I couldn't stop them even though I'm President pro tempore and Presiding Officer in the Senate, but I'm not sure I would have stopped them even if I had the power, which I don't."

"This is anti-Lincoln, anti-war stuff. How can you possibly argue in favor of that?"

"I can't and don't, don't have to. Stephen Douglas and Andrew Johnson, both Democrat senators want to see this issue defeated. It is important that we go on record that there is nothing wrong with The Constitution as it stands, no need for an amendment, or resolution stating that the office is vacant after 30 days, or any other number they arbitrarily choose. Douglas, Johnson, and I feel the same way. In any body, in any organization, the vice president, if there is one, acts in the absence of the president of that body or organization. You do not need any legislation to amplify that simple fact. That is, after all, why you have a Vice President."

"And they want to put that to a vote and defeat it once and for all. Is that what you're telling me?"

"Yes of course."

"And they will succeed?"

"I have no doubt."

"Let's just suppose for a moment that it does pass. Maybe Booth says something or does something that riles the public and Congress acts to protect their seats. What do we do then?"

"I don't know that it matters much. You seem to have forgotten our old friend, Roger Taney. If somehow he and his Supreme Court were to get a hold on this issue there would be all hell to pay. It's no secret that Chief Justice Taney is no friend of Lincoln. Certainly you have not forgotten the Dred Scott decision: Blacks are so inferior they have no rights the white man is bound to respect," he said. "I don't know how he could do it, but if Taney is able to get hold of this, we will be in real trouble. It is clearly a constitutional issue. If Taney were to comment, or the court were to rule, as I expect they would, time would be working against us. Hell, the election's only seven months from now. Taney has fought against racial equality and the slavery issue from the start. You see what I mean. Roger Taney is our real nemesis here."

"Oh I know what you're saying. Remember I'm a lawyer too, and I know Taney well, but there is nothing we can do to stop it. Isn't that awful" Stanton noted rhetorically.

"Reminds me, Mr. Stanton, I meant to ask if you have heard any news from your agents in the South. I recall you telling us that you had Gideon Welles land some of them in Virginia."

"Has not worked out very well. It appears that one team consisting of two New York detectives may have been caught and executed. Some woman from Richmond had a newspaper with a paragraph about it. They caught her here yesterday, but I don't know who she is or anything about her case. Two other teams have returned but had nothing to report except that their gold, our gold, was gone. Stolen they said if you want to believe that."

"Morris' men in Maryland gave up the search after they found Lincoln's watch. You know that story. And one other team in Virginia, I only had four down there, is still out. Have no idea of where they are. May have absconded with the gold. Five hundred dollars in pure gold is a lot of money. Lot of temptation. And, two young men with 1,000 dollars gold between them could go a long way. But what could I do? We had to give them enough to bribe the rebels if they were to have a chance to find the President. I do not think we're going to find him, but we're going to keep trying. I have to go."

The two men on the fourth team that the Secretary of War mentioned were in St. Louis, gambling their way up and down the Mississippi River with no intention of ever returning East.

Being exceptionally cautious, John Surratt and I slowly backed out past the oak tree where Mr. McCreed and the two negroes were hung, to the road out front. The huge mob, many of whom had barely escaped with their lives, watched the house burn to the ground, in silence, then slowly dispersed. We heard them moaning and crying, and smelled the unforgettable odor of burning flesh as we kept walking a little faster now.

We could see Mr. Shoemaker's sign hanging over the wooden platforms that served as a pedestrian walkway all the way to the bottom of the hill. 'Photography Studio' the sign said, but it, like all the other shops in the city, was closed, and would remain closed all the next day while the city reflected on the events surrounding the rumors that I was being held at McCreed's place, and the turmoil that followed with Angus McCreed and 22 others dead. Rufus and Moe, his black helper, were not included in the count.

As we made our way to the back of the studio, John noticed a few steps leading down to a cellar entrance, and decided we would have to spend the night huddled at the bottom of the stairs, or break in. For fear of being seen by people on their way home John simply said "Down here."

He pulled on the handle of the windowless door with no success and knew that he would have to find something to pry it open. At that moment, a voice at the top of the stairs addressed him sharply, "What do you think you're doing down there? Who are you? What do you want?"

"We want some pictures. Who are you? Are you Mr. Shoemaker?"

"Yes of course, but unless you leave immediately I will call for help.

We are closed as you must know. Now are you going to leave or shall I call out?"

"We need help, Mr. Shoemaker" John said emphasizing 'we'. You better come down here and look."

Horace Shoemaker had a great fear of thieves and robbers and no use for beggars so he came down one step, hunched over, and squinted at John and me.

"Oh my God, Lincoln," he gasped. "Oh Jesus, we've got to get him out of here. If they see us they'll string us up. There's a mob out now that's been looking for him. They burned down McCreed's place trying to find him. They believe he was burned up. What is he doing here? How did you get him here?"

"Never mind that now. Let's get him inside before we are seen. Give me the key."

Shoemaker opened the door after fumbling around for the right key and said, "We don't ever use this door. What are we going to do with him now? He can't stay here."

"He is in pretty bad shape Mr. Shoemaker. Look, he is almost unconscious. He has to stay here. He is too ill to move."

"I don't care. I do not want to die or lose my business like McCreed. So he must go."

"Then you go right ahead Mr. Shoemaker. You move him. I will just go on about my business. And when they catch you I'll tell them you did your best, you just wanted to get away from him. And they will believe you of course. They could not possibly believe that you were really trying to hide him from them or worse yet trying to befriend him, taking him back north, would they? I believe you, so you go right ahead and get him out of here now. And, good luck to you, 'cause you are going to need it, a lot of it."

Shoemaker stood staring at me as John ranted on knowing he would have to allow me to stay.

"I guess" he said wearily. "He looks like he is going to die soon anyway, so that could solve part of the problem."

"You married, Mr. Shoemaker?"

"Yes, why? Mrs. Shoemaker, Martha, and I have been married for 29 years next month. Why do you ask?"

"We're going to need her to help care for Mr. Lincoln."

"Oh my God no." Shoemaker exclaimed quickly and emphatically. "It was Martha who spread the word that Lincoln was at McCreed's. She couldn't get around Petersburg fast enough with that news. I know that for a fact. I tried to stop her, to shush her up, but to no avail. I made the horrible mistake of telling Martha that I had seen Lincoln at McCreed's, that John Wilkes Booth wanted me to photograph him, and she did the rest. She hates Lincoln and Yankees and Negroes with a fury, an anger I don't understand because I don't hate people. Like Jesus I try to love 'em, as hard as it is to do that sometimes. But Martha must not know, never know, he is here. I don't want to imagine what would happen to us if she was to find out."

"And her. Her too. Mobs don't stop to listen to reason, or excuses, from anybody, including women named Martha. Keep that in mind Horace it might come in handy some day."

"We can put him in my dark room for now but the only cot I have in the studio won't fit there. Let's put him on the cot and surround it with some boxes."

I held my right hand to my side as John and Horace lifted and dragged me to the cot.

"I'm going home," Horace said.

THURSDAY, APRIL 14, 1864

"Good Lord what's next?" Edwin Stanton said to his visitor, Congressman Schuyler Colfax, the Speaker of the House of Representatives.

A staunch Republican, elected in Indiana in 1862, Colfax tolerated no one who took issue with the President or the war against those traitorous dogs who by seceding from the Union showed their true colors. Traitors one and all. A man with strong conflicting emotions, Colfax was all for fighting to keep the South in the Union, but all for letting them go and die. He simply had no tolerance for slavery or racial divisions and inequity.

Mr. Colfax had shown Stanton a photograph which had been delivered to his office in the House only an hour ago. "You may have one of these, too," he said. That is why I am here."

It was the picture that Lewis took of President Lincoln in bandages, with the severed hand on the table pointing toward Lincoln.

"Is this what we are up against Colfax? What will they do to him next? This photo is bizarre, I don't want to look at it. It is so horrible I can't conceive of what is happening to him. Is that in actual fact his hand? It could be. And that smirk on Booth's face standing behind him. What sort of scurrilous rascal are we dealing with?"

Stanton studied the photograph, looking away at Colfax for an instant, then returning to the picture. "There is something wrong with this photograph" he said. Then, suddenly he jumped to his feet. "Look, that's not his hand. Can't be. The bandages are on this left hand but the hand here is a right hand. They got confused when they turned the hand, so the fingers were pointing at Lincoln. That's not his hand at all. Oh thank God. Do you see what I mean? Look. Look at the thumb. It is a right hand."

"I see what you mean Mr. Secretary. But will others see that too?"

"I don't care" Stanton said, "as long as they have not hurt him."

"Perhaps you should care if others don't see what you saw, and I admit I did not see it, then they will react as you did when first I showed it to you. And then what?"

"What can they do?"

"They can force us to stop fighting for one thing. Suppose they feel that Lincoln or any other man should not have to endure this, this mayhem, this atrocity."

"Enough is enough. Stop this dreadful war. Let them go. We don't want them. Speaking of the South of course. How would you stop or control something like that?"

"I don't know but keep in mind, newspapers cannot print photographs thank heaven, so not everyone is going to see what we've seen. Yes and I know that the press will make a story out of it, especially after Booth's first letter about threatening his life, and the forged signature letter calling for an end to all of this. But we cannot succumb. We're winning. We've got to continue."

And the press did make an issue of it. That very day newspapers in all the major cities headlined the story in big black boldface type:

New photographs show Lincoln in bandages with his hand amputated.

President Lincoln may be facing torture and amputation of body parts by Southern Rebels.

By the time readers got to the story and the fact that it was not Lincoln's hand, and that he had a little smile on his face, readers were overwhelmed by the mere thought that the President could be abused in such a way. They were enraged, and began writing letters to their elected representatives. Woodcut drawings of Booth, and Lincoln's cut off hand were shown and advertised for sale in Harper's Weekly and Frank Leslie's Illustrated News.

"I see no reason why the war should continue…" was the theme of most of the correspondence received in the Capitol during the next several days. It didn't matter that it was not Lincoln's hand. Booth, the propagandist, had made his point dramatically.

Hungry and fatigued Horace Shoemaker didn't bother to eat or speak to Martha when he finally reached home about 10 o'clock. Instead, he fell in bed fully clothed and promptly went to sleep.

Martha was waiting for him in the morning however. She had a lot of questions. "What kept you out so late Mr. Shoemaker?" she asked respectfully, in the manner that many women, north and south, addressed their husbands.

"I am having difficulty controlling my anger woman." he replied in a flat tone of voice. "You have caused a heap of trouble and the loss of a lot of lives by your incessant gossip and mischief. I begged you to not tell anyone about my visit with President Lincoln, because I knew that would stir up trouble. And, now you know it did. You would not listen to me, nor obey, and now Angus McCreed is dead, his house burned to the ground, his business destroyed, and a good many others burned alive. You should repent woman. Your big mouth and picayune brain have brought disaster down upon us. Do you hear me woman do you hear?"

Martha was on her knees now, before her husband, shaking and sobbing, and pleading for forgiveness as Horace left the room without uttering a word. When she calmed down, pushed her hair back and dried her tears, she was finally able to say "What can I do Mr. Shoemaker? How can I make amends? I have made an awful mistake and the Lord will punish me for it. I feel so badly I don't know what to do."

"I will tell you what to do. And this time you had better listen and obey because it can mean life or death for both of us. And I for one do not want to be strung up like McCreed. I doubt if you would enjoy it either."

"I will do anything you ask my husband, anything you tell me to do. I promise. With all my heart I promise to obey."

"All right then, I'll tell you," Horace began, holding his chin and slowly wiping his fingers over his lower lip. "President Lincoln escaped the fire and the mob last night and found his way to my studio. I believe he is still there and may have to stay there for some time. He is a sick man."

Standing in front of her seated husband Martha's eyes grew larger as her mouth fell open but spoke not a word. Stunned, she kept staring at Horace in horror and vacillating between belief and disbelief. "Lincoln," she asked, "is here?"

"Yes, Martha he's here, and you are going to take care of him. I will continue to operate the business without any changes, and help if you or Surratt need me, but we must do all of this without attracting any untoward attention. You understand?"

"Yes. I understand. Who is Surratt?"

"I'm not sure. He is a member of Booth's gang of kidnappers, but beyond that, I don't know. He seems to befriend Lincoln, probably since Booth wants it that way. I don't know. You do whatever he or I say and we will be all right. Surratt and I both want to get him out of here as soon as it's safe to move him. Now you get some things together and bring 'em down to the studio. Not all at once mind you for someone might notice, but secretly, a little at a time. I will say, we should both say, that you are helping me to clean out the cellar, at the studio of course. We need more space, for a bigger dark room. They won't know what that means. You may have to do some cooking there, for the President, but it will have to be light. No smoke and as little odor as possible. And keep whatever you are going to carry under your clothing. No bags or boxes, remember? I have to go now, time to open the store."

"Is he still with us Horace?" Booth asked as soon as he entered the studio in mid-afternoon. "I understand he is ill. Where are you hiding him?"

"In the cellar. There is no place else. But please Mr. Booth please, for the love of God, get him out of here. I don't want him here, don't want to have anything to do with this. Please."

"Steady Shoemaker. I hear you. Now, you listen to me. We are making progress with this plan. We know that thousands of people have written or spoken to their Congressmen up north since the kidnapping began, people who want this damnable war stopped and Lincoln returned safely. That is good news for if the Congress receives sufficient complaints they will act. They are, after all, politicians who want to live another day, to be re-elected. So Lincoln must be kept alive and well, and that may mean keeping him here for a while longer. Do you get my meaning?"

FRIDAY, APRIL 15, 1864

I was rolling ever so slowly and slightly on the cot with my eyes open when Booth approached.

"Pain?"

I nodded 'no' and turned my head away from Booth.

"Has he been like this, John?"

"He has and I am worried because he has a cough and won't eat. She has made some soup for him," he said, looking Martha's way, "but, it don't do no good. I guess Lewis and David got out, that how you found us?"

"You told them where you were going. Good job. Clever the way you all got out of there. Too bad about McCreed."

"What are you going to do for him Mr. Booth? He's getting worse and having real bad dreams. Like last night, he convinced himself and me that he was being hung. I swear it was real. He kept praying that God would care for his soldiers. He told Grant to fight harder, even if he was no longer around. I swear it was like he was actually hanging and talking at the same time Mr. Booth."

"Hallucinating John. Don't concern yourself. I am going back up to Richmond today. Got to see Judah Benjamin again, and Davis, and I know the doctor Sam Mudd is in town, so I will ask him to come down here and take a look at things. All you can do is keep him quiet. I don't know where we can move him so this will have to do. Shoemaker won't like it I know, but he has too much to lose by talking. What about his wife?" "She hates Lincoln, and hates what she is doing but Horace says not to worry, she knows better than to talk. He told me it was her, his wife, that spread the rumors about Lincoln being at McCreed's."

"I know, Horace was there and so were we. Silence is golden, Mr. Surratt. Now doesn't that sound funny coming from an actor?"

"Please have Dr. Mudd come quick Mr. Booth. We ain't got much time."

Descriptions of the now infamous photograph of President Lincoln, Booth and the mysterious hand were now beginning to appear in The New York Daily News, Daily Tribune and The Herald, as well as The Chicago Evening Journal and Chicago Tribune. The public was outraged, far beyond what Edwin Stanton and the Vice

President had foreseen. In New York City, people were assembling outside City Hall, demanding that the mayor speak out for an end to the war. "What have we become?" one shouted. "What has this war done to us? Let them go. We don't want to live with people like that. Stop this crazy war. Live and let live!"

The Mayor, Edward A. Queen refused to appear. "I can't stop this," he told reporters, "It's up to Congress. Write your Congressman."

Few protestors had read beyond the headlines. They visualized the photograph and assumed the worst. "That poor man" they said, "Can you imagine yourself in his place? What would you do? What are they going to do to him next? Why, this is awful. What kind of a country do we live in? This terrible war is not worth it. We should stop it now and let those Southerners do what they want. I've never seen anything like it."

In both the Senate and the House voices were raised to a high pitch. Abolitionists versus moderates. Many yelled out that they did not give a damn either way, just stop this war now. The cost was going to bankrupt the nation. One man hit another with his cane. "I have friends and family in South Carolina sir," he screamed at a Congressman from Illinois, "And they do not own any slaves. Never have. But, they know it is a matter of survival. If there are no slaves to pick the cotton the South, especially South Carolina, will not survive. Their economy, food, shelter, everything depends on their being able to export cotton to England. No slaves means no cotton means the end. Death. And, I am not going to vote for that. Stop the damn war and let the South go. That's the only position that makes sense."

In the Senate they began throwing objects at one another. "What is next Senator?" one man asked another from New Hampshire.

"They going to cut off his ears? How 'bout his nose or toes? There's no end to what they can do and will do. I am disgusted. Slavery will die sooner or later without us intervening. The damn war was a mistake. You can't legislate morality and that's what this is, morals, morality. God, think of all the men who have died to date. On both sides. Do you really believe they accomplished something? Like what? What have we accomplished? What have we done?"

Tempers were rising as ink wells, rulers, pencils, and shoes were thrown at the chair or other Senators who would not be seated. Fist fights were not uncommon.

Finally, after seemingly hours of pounding his gavel to bring order in the Senate Hannibal Hamlin, the presiding officer, succeeded in taking a vote on the Douglas/Johnson Bill. It passed overwhelmingly. Veto-proof, it would, if the House also acted favorably on an identical bill by Archer Owens, go to Vice President Hamlin for signature. Hamlin had made it clear to anyone who would listen that he had no intention of signing it. It would impose an artificial deadline, a deadline that made no sense. He, as the second in line to succeed to the presidency in the event of his death, and otherwise as president in the absence of the President, on a temporary basis only, saw no need to change the status quo.

According to the bill in both houses, the 30 day interval actually began, because of an ongoing military conflict of gigantic proportions, on the first day of the President's absence. Sixteen days of the prescribed 30 had already elapsed. Abraham Lincoln had 14 days in which to return to his office, or lose it. He would become the former president.

George McClellan was beside himself with joy. In 15 days he would have a clear unobstructed road to the Executive Mansion. The U. S. Senate and House of Representatives adjourned 'sine die' late that night and went out and got drunk; the war was nearly over.

Stanton and the rest of Lincoln's cabinet could hardly believe what happened. "Unless we can get him back by April 29 all of our efforts and achievements will have been nullified" William Seward, the Secretary of State, related.

"It's all over. If we haven't been able to do it by now what makes you believe there is the remotest chance of getting him back by April 29?" asked Secretary of the Treasury, Salmon P. Chase.

Stanton despaired. After another round of port, they left his office and went home wondering how, in just two short weeks, the nation they knew and ruled could be turned upside down. "Well it has happened before," Stanton said. "Only a few miles from here. Remember Yorktown, 1781? The world was turned upside down then, too."

SATURDAY, APRIL 16, 1864

For Martha Shoemaker time passed slowly. She didn't want to leave her house nor abandon her near daily visits to friends and neighbors with whom she would discuss a wide range of topics: new recipes, shortages of meat and vegetables, and the war. Lincoln, Grant and Sherman were among her favorite subjects. She considered herself a lady of the Old South, born in New Orleans and educated in the state capital of Louisiana, Baton Rouge. She was very proud of that. She belonged to several clubs in Petersburg, including the most exclusive: 'Southern Ladies Garden Club'.

Only five feet tall, Martha was a bit heavy for her size, but still attractive. Her bright blue eyes were what first attracted her husband. She and Horace met in 1834 at a church supper in New Orleans. Horace and his parents, all born and raised in Louisiana, were vacationing at the time. She married him the following year but didn't move to Petersburg until 1855 when Martha's elderly uncle, Huey, became too old and ill to maintain his photography business. He promised to show Horace how to take pictures, and enjoy a good life in Virginia. Horace learned the business quickly. They had no children.

Martha's father, Norman F. Remoque, dealt in slaves for a number of years, buying and selling whole families, as well as individuals, mostly to plantation owners and overseers along the Mississippi River, all the way up to Natchez. Martha frequently accompanied her father and came to see Negroes as commodities, like cotton and tobacco. Freedom for Negroes was contrary to Martha's way of life. They were slaves, born to be slaves. That was why God made them, she believed. They had no rights and never should. And that meant that Abraham Lincoln and everyone else who followed him or the anit-slavery 'movement', should go to church. Martha was a Christian and took a special delight in telling other Christians at church, or church functions, that Jesus never said anything about freedom for cotton pickers. Neither did Horace. He avoided the subject probably because he knew his maternal grandmother was a Negro. 'Old Mother Gray', long dead, was a family secret that even Martha didn't know, and she knew everything.

She didn't want to leave her house this morning, especially to spend almost the whole day in a cellar with that awful man Lincoln. She didn't care that he was President of the United States of America, or that he was a sick human being. She saw him differently. Lincoln was a vile creature, perhaps the Anti-Christ of which she knew little to nothing about except the expression itself. Martha was never a very good student of anything. She knew how to cook and got along well with her husband but after that she was of little value to herself or anyone else.

With little sleep since Horace scolded her, a lot of time to reflect on what he had said, and what had happened during the past several hours alone in a dimly lit cellar with a very sick man whom she loathed, Martha tried to think of what she could do to earn her husband's respect and return everything to normal. The worst part of the problem she knew was Lincoln himself. How could she remove him from the studio?

She thought of using John somehow or appealing to John Wilkes Booth, whom she found to be unusually handsome and sophisticated even though he hadn't paid the slightest bit of attention to her. But nothing came to mind. John spent most of his time over in a corner of the cellar playing a solitary card game, cleaning his pistol, or napping. He seldom left the studio for fear that someone would notice a stranger in their midst and start asking questions. John had no desire to engage her in conversation. And Mr. Booth was gone. She grew angrier at herself and her dilemma as she, once again, warmed some soup on a small black cast iron coal stove for her patient.

Unintentionally perhaps, the soup began to boil, but I was not aware of that. She dipped a cup in the pot and brought it to me while I was lying on my back, eyes open, watching her. She told me to sit up or it would spill, but nothing about it being too hot to consume. As I reached for the cup and touched it with both hands I instantly realized that it was too hot to hold at the same instant she let go of the handle. As the boiling hot soup spilled from the cup burning both of us, Martha backed away as I quickly began to exit the cot and soup-stained blanket.

"You lumbering old baboon" she shouted at me. "Can't you do anything right? It wasn't that hot. Now, look what you've done. Well you can clean it up Mr. President" she said sarcastically.

"I am sorry madam," I said walking toward her as she backed further away in a frightened state. I was so much bigger than she, and she was alone. I came a few steps closer, intending to hold her scalded hands in comfort, when she turned suddenly, picked up John's revolver, turned to face me, pointed the gun, and fired. All in one motion. One long single moment.

John Surratt heard the shot and came running. It being Sunday with everything nearby closed he had stepped outside for some fresh air in the morning sunlight.

"Good God!" he muttered rushing toward me as I fell back on the cot from the force of the bullet, clutching my right side, blood dripping on the floor, just looking at Martha holding the gun.

Martha said nothing as Surratt wrenched it from her hand. "You little fool. Give me that thing. You could have killed him."

"I believe I frightened her John. I spilled some hot soup and things just got out of hand. I'll be all right. Do we have any towels? I may need a few."

"Where did she hit you sir. Show me."

I pulled my shirt up and looked at the gunshot wound with John, who asked me to turn around.

"I don't see an exit wound Mr. Lincoln. The bullet must still be inside. We are going to need a doctor to do this."

"I'll be all right. Just need some towels, or paper will do. I think one of us ought to reach in and try to find the bullet. I hope it did not hit anything else. I do not know much about anatomy, but I believe there may be some important parts or organs about where that hole is. How will we know?"

"That's why we need a doctor," Surratt said again, and then ordered Martha to go home and bring back some soap and towels, and her husband.

"Go, quickly," he yelled at her. "You better hope he don't die. And get your damn carcass back here fast as you can."

"I do not think it wise for either of us to reach in there for the bullet Mr. Lincoln. We might make this worse by pokin' around. Maybe doctors got some tongs or something they use in cases like this. You know, a tong to grab the bullet and pull it out. You know what I am talking about?"

"Yes I know but I want to lie back John. I feel sort of faint. Where can we find a doctor?"

"I don't know. And, it would be risky to ask anyone around here. Booth said he was going to send Dr. Mudd down, from Richmond, but I don't know how soon to expect him. Maybe Mr. Shoemaker can help. Soon as she brings him back I'll ask. You want to get some sleep?" He pulled the soiled blanket up around my chin.

Horace Shoemaker and his wife returned in less than an hour with several towels and bars of soap tucked under their clothes. He told Mr. Surratt that he was terribly sorry about what happened, and punched his wife in the head as he spoke.

"She's dumb. Stupid, I told her, warned her angrily, but no, she has no brain," he snarled. "What do you do with a woman like this? Nothing but trouble. I'd like to get rid of her before she gets us all hung. Can you believe that? Shooting a man for no cause? Insane! Now, get out of here woman," he said, pausing for breath, "And don't come back. Git."

Surratt shook his head silently and asked about doctors. "None here no more. Except one real old man. They're all in the army. Booth said he knew one in Richmond, though," Horace recalled.

"You better go get him, Horace. Go find Booth in Richmond, probably staying at The American Hotel, one block from the capitol, and tell him what happened. He said he had to see Judah Benjamin and President Davis. Benjamin is the Secretary of State down here so he is probably close to Davis' office. You got to find him. We need Sam Mudd, the doctor, urgently. I do not know how bad Lincoln is so he may die if we can't get him a doctor. Take the next train out, and forget about that wife of yours. I think she heard you this time."

She had. Her head ringing from the blow and insults administered by her once loving husband, deeply resentful of her punishment in the presence of another man, and hating herself for actually shooting another person, Martha went straight to the place where Horace kept his photo supplies and chemicals, mixed a small glass of water with potassium cyanide and drank the whole thing. She fell to the floor, dead, before the glass was empty.

SUNDAY, APRIL 17, 1864

Abraham Lincoln's entire cabinet knew that the legislation which passed both houses of Congress with an overwhelming, nearly unanimous vote, would spell the end of the war unless Lincoln could be found and returned in time, regardless of the constitutionality of it.

If Vice President Hannibal Hamlin vetoed the bill, Congress would override his veto, and the bill would become law without his signature. Then, if challenged and taken directly to the Supreme Court, which because of the nature of the legislation and the time element, looked like a likely possibility, Roger Taney, a pro-slavery, anti-Lincoln Republican, would rally the majority of other eight old men, and rule against any challenge to its constitutionality, and years would pass before the damage could be or would be undone. Meanwhile, Abraham Lincoln is out of office and a place on the November 1864 ballot. George B. McClellan is elected, almost by default, and he declares the South is free to go its own way. The war is over. The Rebels win. They were all depressed by this scenario which they knew was befalling them, but could not develop a plan to stop it or to bring Lincoln back.

"We can only pray that Sherman will take Atlanta before November," Stanton said. "Perhaps the country would allow us to finish the job then, to defeat Lee and restore the Union, no matter what President-elect McClellan might say or do. The South will have been split."

"Perhaps, perhaps, perhaps," Hamlin mocked lightly. "And perhaps McClellan will die of heart failure next week. But, let us all keep our spirits up as we pass the graveyard anyway and hope Sherman can do it. Why not telegraph him to that effect? Tell him it's all up to him. We have to take Atlanta before the election. You think Grant could push him along?"

"He already has gentlemen. If we win, and I still believe we will somehow, it will be Grant and Sherman we have to thank."

"Thank you Edwin Stanton, truly. We all needed that. Let us adjourn for the day now and hope for a better tomorrow." The day before, Saturday, April 16, a report revealed that 46,632 Confederates had been captured since the war began.

Finally, after a frantic search, Horace found Booth, in front of a huge highly adorned mirror at the American Hotel.

"I have looked for you everywhere, Mr. Booth. Mr. Lincoln has been shot."

"Oh? Where? Is he dead?"

"No, alive, but needs a doctor. My wife shot him. John says he needs a doctor right away if he is to live. Can you send Dr. Mudd soon?"

"I have already sent him. He's probably there now. I'm sorry, I have forgotten your name."

"I am Horace Shoemaker, the photographer. Mr. Lincoln is……
"Quiet, man. Be quiet" Booth interrupted. "There are those who would be very interested in anything having to do with 'L'. You understand? 'L'. Now get on with it. You say your wife shot him? Are you serious? Why are you telling me that? This is frankly Mr. Shoemaker, a mystery to me. Why, sir, did your wife shoot 'L'?"

"She was angry. It was an impulse. She is like you. Hates Negroes. And so she hated 'L', the Negro lover."

"I am having difficulty absorbing all of this Mr. Shoemaker. It sounds like a play of some kind. Not a very good play, but intriguing, exciting. She just pulled out her gun and shot him. Is that it?"

"No. She picked up John's gun and shot him. Are you sure Dr. Mudd is on his way? 'L' is a sick man, and no one knows what to do."

"Never fear Shoemaker, Booth is near. I shall accompany you back to Petersburg today. I wish I had been there when 'Mr. L' was shot, not that I could have prevented it, but to have made certain a gun was not available to anyone who might misuse it. Where was John? Why did he leave his gun on a table? And was that not your wife that caused all the trouble we had at McCreed's?"

"Yes. And I scolded her accordingly. I am told that Surratt had stepped outside the door for some fresh air and left his gun behind, because he was concerned that if anyone saw him with a gun they would become alarmed and stir up trouble."

"Your wife must be insane, Shoemaker. Just when my plan to kidnap 'His Royal Highness' is meeting with approval by the administration, you allow your wife to shoot our plan's 'piece de resistance', 'Mr. L'. Pray that he survives Mr. Shoemaker, at least until we have made full use of him. Only this morning our esteemed Secretary of State Judah P. Benjamin told me that he approves of my plan and is trying to convince President Davis, who is vacillating. He is so indecisive at times. Clearly it is vital that we keep 'L' alive."

Dr. Samuel A. Mudd, of Maryland, had been visiting friends in Richmond when Booth called upon him for a diagnosis of Lincoln's physical and mental illnesses. Mudd, a 31 year old M.D. from the University of Maryland, 1858, had four young children and a large prosperous farm and medical practice in Maryland. Upon arriving at the studio, Surratt told him what happened.

"I don't know if there is anything I will be able to do. I will tell you in a few minutes. I know I can't do a comprehensive evaluation, because I would need access to a laboratory with proper medical supplies and equipment to do the job right. All I have here is my doctor's bag, containing a few instruments and potions. I'm going to need some towels John, and some hot water."

I looked at Dr. Mudd and smiled, wanly, as Mudd introduced himself and removed the dirty blanket and blood-soaked towel that John had used to cover the wound yesterday. Mudd wiped away the wet and dry blood that had caked on my body overnight and noticed that a small amount of blood and yellowish body fluid was still seeping out. His hand felt my back and forehead. "Slightly elevated," he said, "and slower pulse, probably from lying still for so long. How much pain are you experiencing Mr. Lincoln?"

"My head hurts Doctor Mudd, but that is my normal condition. The wound throbs all the time but I do not know if that is pain or annoyance. Can you get the bullet out?"

"I do not know where it is sir and frankly do not want to go poking around in there for fear that I might make this worse. The bullet may be serving as a cork as in a bottle of champagne for example. If I remove the cork, the bullet, I may also release something else too: blood, urine, feces or bile may be involved. If the bullet is lodged in a kidney, or your liver, or gall bladder, or colon, we would have an emergency. And, all those body parts are not too far from where the bullet entered."

"Then what do you recommend be done doctor? As you can see, I am in no position to move."

"I am of the opinion Mr. Lincoln that you are going to have to be moved. And, I further believe that you will need a surgeon, a highly skilled and experienced doctor who can open you up and do this right. And we have very little time in which to do it. Your life depends on it Mr. Lincoln. Trust me."

MONDAY, APRIL 18, 1864

Dr. Mudd then told Booth, who had returned from Richmond with Horace Shoemaker, that I was in trouble and needed an operation to remove the bullet, and repair whatever damage may have been done. He said that I could be bleeding inside and we would not know it.

"The only doctor I can think of who has the ability to do this is a fellow named Patrick Dempsey. Pat was my roommate at the University of Maryland Medical School in Baltimore."

"As you know, Mr. Booth, I am not a Lincoln man. I do not like his politics but I am also a doctor and feel that I, we, must do all we can to save his life. As a human being I feel obligated; as a medical doctor having taken the Hippocratic oath I am compelled. Pat Dempsey, the man I recommended, graduated first in our class, and was recognized by the university for his special gifts. As a student, mind you, Pat volunteered to operate on Mr. Chambers, the president of the university."

"It is still talked about in the Maryland medical community. Mr. Chambers apparently had a weak heart which caused him to collapse one day in his office. His wife, or assistant, had the good sense to come to us, in school, and ask for someone, anyone, to help. Dempsey said he would, and Mr. Chambers was opened up in the kitchen of his home. He was unconscious. There was no time to move him. Now, suddenly, here is this 23 year old student operating on a man's heart. My roommate. I was so proud of him I could cry, and did. All of us, his classmates and professors, watched in amazement as he opened Chamber's chest cavity with a kitchen knife, hammer, chisel and wood saw. He had taken control of the situation so quickly no one gave it a thought. Of course, we were all so stupefied watching Pat hold a human beating heart in his hand that we just could not believe it was happening. We had never heard of anything like this."

"He looked up at us and said he would need some towels, surgical knives, clamps, needles, and a lot of bandages."

"Gentlemen, I am going to repair this heart. As you can see, one of the flaps, or cusps, over the opening through which blood enters and leaves the ventricles is not functioning properly. Each ventricle has an inlet flap and an outlet flap that allows blood to flow in only one direction. Four heart flaps prevent backward leaks of blood flowing through the four chambers of the heart."

Asking one of our professors to use the clamps as he indicated, Pat continued on, describing what he intended to do with the malfunctioning flap. "I believe it will be all right now," he said after a few hours, a few quick stitches and a flick of the knife. He used the towels to soak up the fluids that had gathered around the heart, let each of us touch the heart muscle for a few moments, and then said he would close him up; that we should wrap him tightly in bandages.

"We all stood back and applauded."

"That, sir, is a fascinating account of Nineteenth Century medicine at its best. Why Dr. Mudd, you could go on stage with that story. Audiences would besiege you with plaudits of appreciation," Booth said. "You must let me arrange to do that after the war."

"Well Mr. Booth thank you but my only purpose in telling that story about Dr. Dempsey was to convey my conviction that he is the best there is. And he may not be too far from here. I know he is serving with General Lee because he has written to me about the need for doctors in the Confederate Army. Pat joined the Union Army many years ago, shortly after he graduated and passed all his final exams, and was licensed. That really is incredible to my way of thinking, because all that talent could have made him a lot of money in New York City. It was his father who was and may still be a high ranking sergeant of some kind at West Point, who got him to join the Army. His father was a career soldier who had a lot to do with training cadets at the Academy. Wherever Lee is Pat is, because he has so much admiration and respect for Lee. I told him that I considered myself a family doctor, and did not want to leave my wife and kids, three little boys and a girl, to go to war. People at home need doctors too, so I did not feel guilty in not joining up. If you can find Lee Mr. Booth you will find Dr. Dempsey."

"No, Mudd," Booth fired back softly, "You will find General Lee and Dr. Dempsey. I will give you enough money to move around until you find them, and bring Dempsey back. You have done a remarkably good job of convincing me that Dempsey is our man, so good that I expect you will be able to convince Judah Benjamin and ole Jeff Davis himself that you must be allowed through the lines to exhort Lee and Dempsey to send the doctor down here to operate on Lincoln. He does not deserve it in my opinion, but we have little choice in this now." "So," Booth exclaimed as he collected his thoughts, "Get thee back to capital country, Richmond, and don't stop until you have Dempsey, the miracle man, firmly in your grasp at Horace Shoemaker's photography studio. Understand?" he said. "Agreed?"

"Agreed."

Dr. Mudd left my side and went on his way as soon as Booth dropped several gold coins in his hand and wished him 'Godspeed'. His plan was to get a letter from President Davis ordering or beseeching Robert E. Lee to release Dr. Dempsey on a special mission of mercy.

TUESDAY, APRIL 19, 1864

Major General George McClellan did his best to convince fellow Democrat Stephen Douglas that Abraham Lincoln should be declared dead in the absence of any news to the contrary, but Douglas, winner of the Illinois Senate race against Lincoln following the Great Debates of 1858, would have none of it.

"I'm sorry George, I believe Mr. Lincoln is still alive, else we would have heard otherwise. I believe the country knows that he is trying to preserve the Union, and is still with him. We cannot stop now. How could we possibly justify the deaths of so many thousands of men, after three years of war, were we to cut and run now? Do you realize that is a very old expression, George? Goes all the way back to Boston, in 1707. Well, we are not going to cut and run. Don't you see momentum alone will carry us soon to victory, no matter what may befall the President? It is beyond politics, George. Politics is the art of getting and keeping what you want. That is the true definition of politics. And we must understand that. You would think in this case we would transcend politics, because everyone wants the same thing: peace and tranquility. But that is not the way it works. Politics are present whenever there are two or more people. On a small boat, for example, two men at sea, with nothing to eat but an orange are in a political situation. Who gets the orange? How? It may at that point represent life or death. The politics involved in deciding what to do with the orange illustrate my point. There are many different ways, but all political, of handling the orange problem. But it is politics, is it not? In your case, George, all we have is your personal ambition, the desire to replace the man who fired you. The desire to become the next President of the United States. You are out to get and keep what you want. And that is the definition of politics: the art of getting and keeping what you want. He fired you, I might add, on two occasions, as if you didn't know, because you would not fight, you just would not lead your army to fight. Do you recall that President Lincoln said that you 'had the slows'? Or recall that he asked if he could borrow the Army from you since you weren't using it?"

On the return to Richmond Dr. Mudd decided that he would bypass meetings with Judah Benjamin and President Davis, and try to find General Lee's headquarters instead. That would save some time he reasoned, and time now was working against him. Lincoln needed an operation, and that could not be delayed. Meetings in Richmond might take a whole day or more. Mudd however did not know where Lee might be, only that he was fighting north of Richmond someplace, fighting to stop the Yankee Army advance.

He asked the conductor on the Richmond, Fredericksburg & Potomac Railroad, and was told there was a lot of activity up in the Fredericksburg area, that the train would only go as far as Thornsburg, a little town about 15 miles south of Fredericksburg. After that, Mudd was told, he would be on his own.

He began to wish he had a letter from Jefferson Davis when he saw all the soldiers, wagons and artillery as he got off the train. Thousands of men carrying rifles and backpacks were marching behind the cavalry, men on an endless line of horses. Tents, boxes of ammunition, and thousands of barrels of gunpowder were stacked everywhere.

The first man in uniform he asked told him to see the captain, over there.

"Where can I find General Lee, Captain? I am a doctor and want to volunteer my services."

"There is some fighting a little farther north, doctor. You will probably find him up there if you can find a way to get up there. Wait, doctor, wait. I think I know how you can do it. See that small wagon by the ammunition dump? The white one. I think that's carrying medical supplies. If you can get a ride from them you will get close to General Lee. Good luck!"

A half hour later Dr. Mudd was on his way to the front. The driver told him that Major Dempsey was the best surgeon they had. "He can cut a leg off faster than any of the other two doctors. In seconds" he said. "Before you know you lost it it's gone. Same with arms. Don't have time to scream" he added admiringly.

"You gonna give 'em some help doc?"

"Don't know yet. Not even sure they want me."

"Don't know what we'd do without Major Dempsey. We all know about him 'round here and they ask for him to do it if they're still awake and can talk."

The bloody parts of unknown numbers of Confederate and Union soldiers were piled high on both sides of the large tent where Major Pat Dempsey and another doctor, Captain Albert Banes, were amputating the parts as fast as others could lift or help lift them to the operating table. Legs, arms, feet, hands were thrown to the ground in seconds. There were screams, loud and heart stopping, before, during, and after the saws ripped through the torn mangled bloody flesh and bone. But a pony glass or two of whiskey, and a smooth piece of hard wood to bite down on helped stifle the pain and muffle the cries in most cases. Only four months ago, at Fredericksburg, 27,000 Union soldiers had attacked Rebel forces relentlessly. Over 14,000 men fell, dead; 8,000 Yankee, 6,000 Confederate. By the time many of the Johnnie Rebs and captured Yankees reached Lee's hospital tents and Dr. Dempsey, they were suffering from gangrene. But Dempsey and the other doctors took them as they arrived: first come, first served. No favorites, the same as they did up north. Mudd stood and cried as he watched. He stepped outside after a few minutes to get control of his emotions and chastise himself silently for falling victim to a human reaction. I am a doctor, he told himself, and doctors have no room for pity or sorrow in the process of saving lives.

Back in control, he re-entered the tent, walked up behind Dr. Dempsey and said, "Dr. Sam Mudd reporting for duty Sir." Pat turned his head and looked directly into Mudd's eyes. "It's a hell of a duty Sam, but we've got to do it. What brings you here? You join up?" All the while he continued talking without missing a stroke of the knife or saw. Other attendants quickly applied a tourniquet and removed the amputee from the table.

"Al, I will be right outside if you need me." "Sam," he said, removing his heavy blood-streaked leather apron. "I sure didn't expect to see you here. It's been a while since I saw you last. Let's see, 58, 64, God. Six years?"

"Six long years."

"I need a rest Sam. This has been going on too long, three years now. God, I don't think about them anymore. Our amputees. It is just an old routine now. Poor bastards. They'll have to live with it for the rest of their lives. You have to feel sorry when some poor guy loses all four, arms and legs. And we've had a lot of them. Imagine that? No arms no legs. Now how you going to live like that?"

"I don't know. Let's talk about something else. Anything else, and hope this is over soon."

"It will be, Sam. Grant won't stop like those other generals did. He just keeps comin'. He is suffering some pretty heavy losses too, but he can afford it. They got a lot more to call on than us. It won't be long now, but don't tell General Lee I said that. He is doing all he can. How's the family Sam? How many kids you got?"

"Four, and I miss them. Came down here with John Wilkes Booth to save the Confederacy and now I want to go home. You ever get married Pat?"

"No, I guess I should have. Came close years ago at West Point. Must have been '60 or '61, just before Fort Sumter. We had a reception and dance at the officer's club. New Year's Eve. That was it. December 31, 1860. Seems like a long long time ago. For those of us who had no guest, the senior officers usually invited their daughters, or granddaughters, you know, and friends. One girl, Miss Charlotte Parker was her name, from Richmond, took my breath away, Sam. She was so pretty I was afraid to ask her to dance, at first. I knew she would say no. But she did not. I believe she told all those other fellows no but not me. We danced until the club closed and the chaperones told us we had to leave. We lost track of each other after that. Don't know why. Just did. She probably wasn't interested in me. Who wants to marry a soldier?"

"You are a doctor Pat. And, a good one. Did she know that?"

"Don't recall. You think she is waiting for me to call Sam?"

"Well you should try. Who knows, love has a funny way of showing up when you least expect it. Which by the way brings me to the point. The true reason I am here."

"Can you make it short Sam? I have got to get back in there. Lee is expected to visit us sometime this afternoon, and we've got a lot of work to do."

"Robert E. Lee?"

"None other Sam. You know him?"

"No but I have to talk to him."

Dr. Mudd went on to tell Pat about Booth and President Lincoln's kidnapping and shooting.

"We need you Pat to save Lincoln's life. You are the only one who can do it. That's why I have to talk to General Lee. As important as these poor fellows are to you, and to him, it's actually more important that we save Lincoln. If he should die we have lost any possibility of ending this war on our terms. And should he die I believe the South would suffer badly, under any President, if we were the people who killed him. Like Jesus, the people held the Jews responsible for his death, and the poor Jews have suffered ever since. We can't let it happen Pat, can't even take the risk of it happening. Should the South lose the war and we are held accountable for the death of Abraham Lincoln, you all might just as well move to China. The North would never forgive us. Don't you see Pat? We need you. Now!"

"I understand Sam. And agree with you. But it is up to Lee. He is the only one who can decide this, and would you believe Dr. Mudd, here he comes."

With two other officers on horseback, General Lee approached the hospital tent and dismounted. Exchanging brief salutes and informal greetings, Lee walked into the tent and up to the soldier on the operating table.

"What is your name son?"

"Lew Sir," the boy said trying to raise himself in respect. "Lewis Carter, Private, Tallahassee, Florida Sir."

"You are a long way from home Lewis. And, we are all proud of you. You get some rest now. The doctors will take good care of you, then you can return home as a hero. Good luck son."

General Lee spoke to several of the men waiting their turn, then motioned to doctors Dempsey and Banes to join him outside.

"We are going to have to fall back again soon gentlemen so be prepared, if that is possible. You are doing an excellent job here, and I want you to know that our country appreciates it. We need more like you. But try to get some rest."

"General Lee I would like to present my college roommate, a gentleman from Maryland, Doctor Samuel A. Mudd."

Lee greeted Mudd and asked him if he would like to work for the Confederate Army. "We need men like you doctor."

Mudd thanked him for the offer and went on to describe his mission, just as he had to Pat Dempsey moments before. "Time is critical General. If we are going to save him we must act now, and Dr. Dempsey is the only man who can handle this. He has the experience, and above all, the talent." Mudd proceeded to tell General Lee how Dempsey saved Mr. Chamber's life at the University of Maryland.

"We cannot lose Lincoln General. It could become a political catastrophe."

Lee glanced at him quizzically but said nothing. "I understand Doctor Mudd, but we need doctors desperately."

The three men looked at each other. Then Doctor Mudd broke the silence. "I believe I can do this General Lee. I know I could never replace Dr. Dempsey but I would certainly try. If Pat, Doctor Dempsey, left now, he could be in Petersburg tomorrow."

"I have to agree with you Doctor Mudd. It is absolutely imperative that we save, or at least try to save, President Lincoln. As you so diplomatically implied a moment ago, it is probably in our own best interests as ironic as that may be. It is therefore, my wish Dr. Dempsey that you leave now on this mission of mercy. I will write your orders at once, and get you sufficient money for the trip. Doctor Mudd can tell you where to go, and start his duties as soon as he thinks he is ready. You are now a Captain in the Army Doctor Mudd. Congratulations."

"Thank you General. And to expedite this, I am going to give Doctor Dempsey the gold that Booth gave me when I left to find you this morning."

"Keep this up Doctor Mudd and I just may promote you to Colonel. Goodbye gentlemen."

WEDNESDAY, APRIL 20, 1864

After introducing the newly commissioned Captain Samuel Mudd to Doctor Banes and asking one of his best orderlies, Sergeant Billy Johnson, to accompany him to Petersburg on a secret mission, Dr. Dempsey received his orders from General Lee's adjutant and left the encampment.

He hoped to take a train but knew that might not be possible now, at 8 p.m. He told Sergeant Johnson to borrow the medical supply wagon in case. And that is the way it happened. It rained almost the entire way to Richmond, where sentries along the wet muddy streets in the city watched them pass without interruption. Everywhere they looked, people were sleeping wherever it was dry. Refugees.

Dr. Dempsey examined me as soon as he arrived at the studio, and told Horace Shoemaker and John that he would have to operate. But he would need a bigger and better facility.

"We will have to move him of course. But where?" he asked.

"We only had two doctors in town that I knew of, Major. Dr. Hughes who only made house calls and died long ago, and Dr. Jones. Noah Jones. He was about your age, killed at Gettysburg they say, almost a year ago. His place is about a mile from here, not far from where I live. Big white house. He left a widow, Annabelle. Nice lady. She still lives in the house they built. Big, nice place. And he did operate come to think, in the front part of the house. Called it his clinic. That is about all we have. I'll take you out there, to Doc Jones' place if you want to see it, that is if Annabelle wants you to see it. She may have other plans but I know she is still there. Like I said we are almost neighbors."

Knowing there were no military medical facilities south of Richmond, Dempsey accepted the offer to ride out to Dr. Jones'.

"Mrs. Jones my name is Patrick Dempsey. I am a surgeon in General Lee's Army and would like to talk with you on a confidential matter. I believe you know Mr. Shoemaker. He told me that you lost your husband last year at Gettysburg. I'm truly sorry Mrs. Jones, about your loss. It must have come as a terrible shock. I was there at Gettysburg but, unfortunately, didn't know your husband. We had quite a few doctors then."

"Won't you come in Dr. Dempsey? And Mr. Shoemaker. I am so glad to meet you and am truly grateful to you, Mr. Shoemaker, for bringing him here. Would you gentlemen like some refreshments?"

"Thank you Mrs. Jones, I would enjoy a little tea if you will join me. Would you excuse us for a bit Mr. Shoemaker. I may have to get into some confidential military matters which are restricted by military edicts of one kind or another."

"Yes, of course Major. But you should know that it was not me who spread those rumors or shot Mr. Lincoln. It was my wife. And, she is dead now. She poisoned herself out of remorse for having shot Mr. Lincoln accidentally."

"Let us discuss that in private later Mr. Shoemaker. My request for confidentiality is purely routine, it has nothing to do with you or your missus."

"Then I will wait outside Major. I believe I understand."

"Did I hear him correctly Doctor? Has President Lincoln been shot?"

"He has indeed Mrs. Jones, and that is why I am here. Not very many people know that Mr. Lincoln is still alive and in Petersburg, only a mile from here."

"I did hear a rumor a while back that Mr. Lincoln was here in our town, but this all gets so confusing that I find myself losing interest in it. Would you be so kind as to enlighten me? It runs in my mind that the actor, John Wilkes Booth, had kidnapped Mr. Lincoln, and had him down here somewhere. Are you now telling me that he, Lincoln, is my neighbor? How charming" she laughed lightly. "The President of the United States of America lives next door to little Annabelle," she said sweetly as she fluttered her left hand and laughed again, flirting with her new friend, Doctor Patrick Dempsey. He laughed too.

"It is so nice to talk to you Mrs. Jones. I have not seen a woman, much less talked to one, for so long now that I was starting to believe that the whole world was populated only by soldiers. Now in just a few minutes you have changed all that. And I do appreciate it Ma'am. I really do. I am glad to know, once again, that there are some beautiful people in this country, not just ugly Yankees.

"Why thank you for that marvelous compliment Doctor Dempsey. But you need not call me "ma'am". Makes me feel like I'm some old matron that people have to look up to. And I am not like that at all, Doctor Dempsey. May I call you Pat or Patrick sir? You may call me Anna or Annabelle, or anything you want."

"All right, but please do not call me 'sir'. That has the same connotation as 'ma'am' don't you think? We could always call each other 'Ma' and 'Pa'," he shrugged and smiled. She laughed again.

"Well, in all seriousness Mrs. Jones, Anna, President Lincoln is your neighbor now, but may be your house guest tonight." Dempsey went on to tell about the lynch mob at McCreed's, the shooting, and the need for an operation.

"You have no obligations in this Anna, but I know it would make a difference if I had a decent place to operate, and Shoemaker's photo shop won't do."

"That is how Noah, my husband, felt too. When I had this home built for us, I knew he needed proper space and all to operate. Of course you may use it. But you must also agree to stay here, you and your staff, and not at that hotel downtown, The Virginia. Does that sound fair and reasonable?"

"Very much so. More than I had hoped for. All of this has to be private, Anna. You understand that? Lincoln's life and ours would be in jeopardy if word got out."

"You can trust me and count on me for whatever help you need Patrick. I fully understand what you are saying and attempting to do. Would you like to see Noah's clinic? He was very proud of it."

Dempsey was impressed with what he saw and said so. He told Mrs. Jones that he would bring the President, his orderly Sergeant Johnson, and one of the kidnappers, John Surratt back as soon as he could, that he would like to operate yet today.

"Now," he concluded, "do you need anything to make this happen Anna? Any supplies, help or protection? I have plenty of money, gold, if you need any cash."

"Thank you Patrick. I have no need for money or gold. I don't know what to do with what I have. My daddy left me the plantation, 30,000 acres of cotton in Natchez, Mississippi, and all the slaves, have to be 150 or more, plus a mansion overlooking the river. Lovely home Patrick, but what good is it? England does not want our cotton anymore, and the slaves may be freed if we lose this damn war, so all I will have is a big three legged mule. Thank God he also left me with a little liquid money, too, so I think we will be, I will be, all right."

Joining an unhappy photographer, Dempsey got on Horace Shoemaker's wagon and returned to move his patient.

"We are going to bring him here, Horace. I am pleased beyond measure you suggested this place. It should work out fine. What do you know about Noah and Annabelle Jones? Did he go to school around here?"

"In Charlottesville, Major. University of Virginia Medical School. Good student, I hear. Came from a poor family but had the calling. You ever get the calling?"

"It was so long ago Horace. I honestly don't remember. I was born with it I suppose. I always wanted to help animals that were injured, or looked like they needed help. You know, a dog or cat that got in the way of a wagon wheel, or an animal that someone shot, just for practice, or fun. I would try to make them whole again. What about her? Where is she from?"

"Annabelle is a foreigner, from Mississippi. She built that place we just visited, to keep Noah happy. Doc Jones was a hell of a nice fellow. Like I said, about your age, height, weight. He loved her as much as she loved him. Don't know why, because she could buy the whole city of Petersburg, and he didn't even own a horse. No kids. Don't know why. Actually they didn't have much time together maybe. They were only married for a year or two before he volunteered. It was tragic. Gettysburg. Did I hear you say you were there?"

"It was awful, Horace. Awful. I did not know Doctor Jones, but that is not unusual. Like the Yankees, we had several field hospitals on, or quite near, the battlefield, and no time to socialize. It was not pretty. It never is. And we have not seen the end of it yet. Wait 'till they get here."

I was in pain, clutching my cot when Dr. Dempsey returned. Sergeant Johnson and John Surratt let the cot act as a stretcher as they loaded me gently into the white Army Medical Wagon. Dempsey stayed with me inside as we made our way to Dr. Jones' clinic, the Petersburg Executive Mansion. John smiled when Doctor Dempsey used that expression for the first time.

"If anybody should ask what the white supply wagon is doing here Horace, tell them the Army is requisitioning some chemicals. That ought to satisfy them. So long as no one knows what we are really doing we will be safe. You too. If you have a bill for all your help, and food and staples, Horace, you should note them and give it all to me later on. I think the government should pay you for this."

Dr. Dempsey told me what he intended to do, and why, as we approached the clinic. "I am going to try to hypnotize you Mr. Lincoln. Since we have no chloroform or ether here, it is the only way I know of eliminating pain. I have never tried this before so I cannot promise that you will not feel anything. This could be very painful. But it must be done. I will do my best, of course, to avoid prolonging the operation. But until I see what needs to be done, I cannot make any guarantees. And I must tell you, sir, I cannot even guarantee that it will be a success. Only the Lord knows that, so a prayer now and then might help. You might say one for me too. I will be too busy trying to decide what to do and how to do it."

Dempsey insisted that I drink the whiskey Annabelle found in one of the locked cabinets, and bite down hard on a five inch long, half inch diameter oak bit, when and if I was in pain.

I said nothing, just lay helpless with my arms and legs tied securely to the operating table, until I saw the knife in Dr. Dempsey's hand. Then, in a low voice, said "God bless you", and closed my eyes.

With Sergeant Johnson on one side and John on the other, both with towels, and instruments on trays, Dr. Dempsey used a razor sharp surgical knife to cut a flap of skin from just below the right nipple, over to the center of my body, down almost to my navel and back over to my side, several inches directly below the point where he made the first incision. The bullet had entered at the center point of that skin door, as Sergeant Johnson called it. Quickly and firmly, with both hands, Dempsey gripped the skin at both corners and pulled it steadily up and over toward him, holding the flap in place with clamps affixed to the operating table. All that seemed to take less than a minute, and I felt no pain.

Dempsey did not see the bullet, but could see part of the path it followed. Without hesitating, he began to probe the hole with his left hand, taking several minutes before exclaiming with a professional mixture of joy and relief, "I have it." Gently pulling his hand out, he held the bullet up.

"You were lucky, Mr. Lincoln, or blessed. It did not hit your lung, spine, colon, or anything else that I could feel, just finally hit a muscle and stopped."

I lay still, my eyes closed, but seemed to grasp what the doctor was saying. A barely perceptive nod and gulp revealed that I understood the significance of Dempsey's diagnosis.

"You have some other problems, however; perhaps the reason why you have not been feeling well."

Doctor Dempsey watched me intently as he spoke, noticing that I was not biting down on the oak bit or manifesting any pain, which under normal circumstances would be almost too much to bear. My eyes closed, I appeared to be asleep, so he concluded, at least for now, that I was either a stoic, or in a hypnotic trance. On our way to the Petersburg Executive Mansion, Dempsey had asked me to count down slowly from 1,000, while watching him move his arm and pocket watch slowly back and forth, like a pendulum. As I counted, Dempsey would match the number, in a low voice, with the word 'sleep'.

Amateurish, Dempsey thought, but worth a try. He had read all he could find about hypnosis, but didn't know if he could do it successfully. He still wasn't sure.

"Mr. Lincoln, I am going to remove your appendix and gall bladder. Both are enlarged and should come out. The appendix looks like it is about to burst and, if that were to happen, you would be in serious trouble. Were it to burst, the rupture would release the contents into your abdominal cavity causing peritonitis. That would kill you. Since you are also suffering from cholecystitis, an inflammation of the gall bladder, you probably have gallstones. This is also a serious matter, but we can remedy that now. Might as well, don't you think? We will do a cholecystectomy. Just think, all that is not going to cost you anything. So just lie there and sleep. When I say 'wake up', you will not be in pain. Indirectly, Mrs. Shoemaker may have saved your life."

Annabelle Jones stood on a little platform closely overlooking the operation, hearing every word Dr. Dempsey uttered. But Patrick Dempsey, other than observe my facial features from time to time, never looked up.

He continued to clamp and cut and sew, until he got to the appendix. "This could be messy, gentlemen," he said, feeling my enlarged colon. "I am going to have to remove that worthless accessory we call the appendix, without nicking the colon to which it is attached."

He finished in a few minutes, wiped his brow and asked for some iodine.

"If he is feeling anything," he said, looking into my eyes, as I held onto the oak wood bit with my teeth, "this is really going to do it."

Whereupon he began to paint over the bullet hole, and wherever he had cut, with a small glass rod. "I read about this, too. Suppose to keep things clean, disinfected. Let's close him up now, Billy, I am getting tired." I had been on the table for four hours when Doctor Dempsey pulled the flap of skin back in place, began to sew, asked Johnson to paint the whole area, and sat down.

Annabelle applauded. "I am truly impressed Patrick. You are better than Noah."

THURSDAY, APRIL 21, 1864

Doctor Dempsey waited until John and Billy Johnson wrapped me tightly in bandages around my torso before waking me up. Dempsey was convinced now that I had been in a trance because I did not say anything about pain. I asked if it was over when I saw the bandages and was told to go back to sleep, the operation had been a success.

Without thinking much about it, Dempsey asked Sergeant Johnson to deliver a message to a Miss Charlotte Parker in Richmond. "I have lost the address, Billy, but you should be able to find her. Find her father or mother's house and you will see her. I will give you a note to give to her and show whomever my orders from General Lee. You cannot tell anyone who our patient is Billy, but you can say it is important. We need someone to care for him around the clock. So if she wants to bring a friend along, that is fine, just come now, return here with you, today. As I said, this is important and will not wait. I met Miss Charlotte at West Point a few years ago, and only hope that she is still unmarried. Go now, Sergeant. Take the Richmond & Petersburg train because I want to keep the wagon near in case of an emergency. Mr. Surratt will take you to the station," "I believe," he said, looking at John who dropped his head slightly in assent, as if to say, "He is my prisoner, but I will leave him because I trust you."

They hadn't been gone long when John Wilkes Booth arrived at Annabelle's home and introduced himself to Dr. Dempsey and Annabelle, neither of whom had ever met Booth, but had seen him perform. Both were impressed with his appearance and demeanor, particularly Annabelle, who was very much taken by the handsome actor.

"Oh Mr. Booth, I am so delighted to make your acquaintance. I want to welcome you to what I understand is now referred to among our friends as 'The Petersburg Executive Mansion', and invite you to be my guest for as long as you care to stay. You have always been my favorite performer. I have seen several of your plays, and wondered what you would be like off stage. I must say that in just these last few minutes, since your dramatic arrival on that big black stallion out there, you have already captured my heart. I am completely captivated."

Somewhat uncomfortable with her lengthy sentiment, Booth merely smiled an acknowledgement of the accolade, bowing graciously.

"Thank you my dear. I am hardly worthy of such compassion."

Patrick Dempsey watched, amused but awestruck, as Annabelle the obsequious lost him forever.

Booth turned to him after his bow and asked, "Will he live doctor?"

"Probably."

"That may be a problem. The Northerners do not seem to understand that his life hangs in the balance. I had hoped, and planned, on their paying the price, the ransom if you will, to win him back. I believe it was Richard the Lion Hearted, was it not, who was saved when his ransom was paid after he was kidnapped while returning from one of the crusades? Well why damn it, can't those nigger-loving politicians up North do the same? Have they not read Shakespeare? Don't they understand that there is an historical precedent?"

"I am not fascinated by politics Mr. Booth, so I cannot comment intelligently. My only concern is that Mr. Lincoln recover his health. That is the extent of my responsibility. Dr. Mudd asked me, on your behalf as I recall to come here and operate, if need be, on President

Lincoln. He said it was crucial Lincoln's life be saved. Beyond that I dare not go. We are at war, and Mr. Lincoln is the Commander in Chief of the U. S. Army. Yet here I stand, possibly having saved his life, at the request of none other than Robert E. Lee, Lincoln's chief enemy, the principal reason we have lost so many fine men on both sides. From my own experience operating on these men Mr. Booth, they do not know what they are fighting for. They are not slave owners. They do not give a fig about states' rights or Federal Government. Most of them can hardly spell their name much less read or write. They are farmers, most of them. They are poor and vulnerable. Someone told them it was a glorious cause. I do not know what that means but their friends joined up so they decided they would too. I am hardly better off than they. I too was poor. My father was a career soldier and that meant hardship. I am not really sure why I am here. Only because General Lee was so inspiring, so eloquent, so convinced that Virginia was right, and the Federal Government wrong, did I decide to follow him, rather than my own father, Master Sergeant Michael Dempsey, a Yankee soldier, still on active duty. It is very confusing to me Mr. Booth. I really do not know how to respond to your avowal."

"I am sorry doctor. I thought you understood. Perhaps, probably, it is me. I want so desperately, for the states to be allowed to go their own way that I vowed I would stop at nothing to make that a reality. We are the eleven states of the Confederacy, united in the sense that we oppose domination by other states, or too strong a central federal government. We believe in the rights of the states, Virginia, North and South Carolina, Georgia, all the rest, to act in their own best interests, and to hell with moral vigilantes who see the Negro as an equal. All men were not created equal doctor, and your skill and ability, attest to that. Negroes are slaves. God made them that way. I did not invent slavery, we did not invent it. It always was and will be. The Negro is simply not our equal. Surely you understand that?"

"I cannot deny that slavery is probably as old as time Mr. Booth, but you cannot deny that we have progressed far beyond what our forefathers knew and experienced, only 50 years ago. We are more civilized than they. We know that, but for the color of their skin, the black man is exactly the same as the white man. There is no other difference physically or mentally. Economically, however, I grant you there were and are important differences.

The blacks, in Africa, not unlike American Southerners today, wanted to be left alone, to act as tribal units, in their own best interests. No Federal Government, no moral critics from outside their realm. And then when the white man, at some point in time, realized that the Negroes were behind in commerce and trade, and all that money can buy, they began to take advantage of them."

"Stop, doctor. Stop. Enough said. You must know by now that I hate these blacks, Negroes, niggers. They are inferior. And, Abraham Lincoln loves them. That is why he may still have to go. He may still be of some use to us. Time will tell. But in the interim, be on notice that my fellow conspirators and I will be watching you carefully. He is our prisoner, doctor, and that supersedes his status as your patient. I assume you can understand that."

Turning to Annabelle Jones, who had listened to the entire debate, Booth asked if he could partake of any liquid imbibement from Kentucky that she might happen to have in her wine cellar.

Flattered beyond her most forbidden dreams, Annabelle said, "Come with me, Mr. Booth, "I am yours, to stay or slay."

Later in the afternoon, as Booth and Annabelle were enjoying an occasional nip of fine Kentucky bourbon, exchanging ideas for various cocktails, many of which had not been invented yet, and friendly bonhommies, Sergeant Johnson entered the room and asked for Major Dempsey.

"Upstairs, dear," Annabelle replied. "With your President."

"The ladies are outside major. Do I bring them in?"

"Yes of course Billy. I take it you found Miss Charlotte?"

"Finally, major. She sort of found me. Soon as I told her mother you were looking for her, she came out and asked me if you were from New York. I don't know where she was hiding, but she sure knows who you are."

"I will be down in a moment Billy. The President is restless and probably hungry, but I want to say a few words when he awakes. It has been a difficult time for him and he deserves to know what has happened."

When, after several minutes telling Mr. Lincoln of the removal of a few of his body parts, Doctor Dempsey went downstairs, Miss Charlotte Parker was a bit peeved. "Did you not want us Patrick?" she asked, quickly followed by an introduction to Miss Peggy Ann Post, a cousin of Charlotte Parker, and one for whom Miss Charlotte felt a great deal of simpatico. Miss Peggy was also the daughter of an erstwhile Union officer, killed at Antietam in 1862.

"I have told Peggy of our dance at West Point. She so enjoys our happiness."

"Anna, Mr. Booth, I should like to present two young ladies who have agreed to care for President Lincoln at all times during his recuperation. Miss Charlotte Parker, to my left, and Miss Peggy Ann Post. They will nurse Mr. Lincoln back to health, if that is possible, and report to me as to his progress. Both Miss Charlotte, and Miss Peggy, are the daughters of Confederate patriots, officers in the C. S. Army. Miss Charlotte, Miss Peggy Ann, this is Mrs. Annabelle Jones, who has made her home here available to the Army, and none other than the famous actor, John Wilkes Booth, of whom you have heard so much about and witnessed on the stage."

Annabelle quickly welcomed the girls, and told them they had the run of the house, and if they wished to make a meal for themselves or Mr. Lincoln, to direct Mamie, her Negro cook in the kitchen, to just do it, that Mamie could cook anything they wanted.

Charlotte asked Booth if he felt comfortable play acting. "Do you really believe who you are?"

"I am who I am, miss." he replied. "Tell me I am Napoleon, and I will tell you I can see the sun rise at Austerlitz; that I will burn Moscow. And I will, if you let me. Say that the Prussians are coming, at Waterloo, and I will say, 'Oh God no, it is the end. It is all over.' And, it is. The end. Finis. Does that answer your question?" He smiled then, and turned to Annabelle, "Such are the ways of the hoi polloi."

In Washington meanwhile, Edwin Stanton bemoaned the fact that he had heard nothing from any of his operatives in Virginia. "I feel like going there myself," he told his secretary. "No news is bad news." Various rumors had floated about concerning Mr. Lincoln, who may have been a victim of a fire at some embalmer's, but nothing after that. At one point he directed the telegraph office to offer an exchange of prisoners. "We will release 1,000 men in exchange for President Lincoln," Stanton telegraphed to Jefferson Davis in a desperate attempt to bring Lincoln home. There was no reply. Newspapers all over Union states were speculating on Lincoln's whereabouts, and what would happen to the nation were the legislation, just passed, to become law. Would Vice President Hamlin become our president? Would he end the war? Would George McClellan be the next president? How would the South be treated after the war? How should it be treated? These, and many other questions, troubled people who followed the war. What about Lincoln? Is he alive? Where? Endless questions were asked of the newspapers, and the politicians. No one knew.

Then suddenly, late Friday afternoon, Stanton received a telegram from Petersburg.

To: Edwin Stanton
Washington, D. C.

April 21, 1864

Mr. Lincoln is in my care but not for long. This war must be stopped and the southern states given their freedom or your president will pay the price. No more obfuscations. End the war now or he will become a sacrificial lamb.

Booth

Attempting to keep the President alive, Stanton ordered an immediate response:

To: Booth
Petersburg, Virginia

U. S. Congress has passed a bill nearly unanimously, declaring office of President of U. S. vacant after 30 days.

This is first step in meeting your demands. Vice President Hamlin will become new executive. If President Hamlin says war is over, we expect to see Mr. Lincoln alive and well. Is that agreed?

Stanton, U. S. A.

There was no reply.

Fuming, after waiting more than three hours, Stanton left his office for a meeting with Hamlin. He showed the Vice President both telegrams and said, "You must make a statement. Lincoln's life depends upon it. Keep it open. Say I will decide to end the war based on the facts and figures. How many men have been killed or injured, on both sides? How many more must die? That sort of thing. Or say you will open the issue of continuing the war for public discussion and approval. You know, and Booth knows, the public is fed up with the war. They want to stop it. His life is at stake. We have to buy time."

I was hungry when I awoke. Peggy Ann went down to the kitchen and asked Mamie if she would prepare something for the man upstairs.

"What man upstairs?"

"Mr. Lincoln, I believe," Peggy replied.

"Well, he like chicken soup?"

"I believe so, Mamie. Make some soup. I will help. What do you want me to do?"

"I make da soup, honey. You jus' sit still. Nice and quiet. I make da soup."

In a few minutes, Peggy Ann brought a tureen of hot chicken soup upstairs. Patiently, she served it to me, spoon by spoon.

"You are a lifesaver, Miss," I said. "Did you make this?"

"No, Mr. President," Peggy said. "Mamie the cook made it, and I think she knows what she's doing, don't you?"

I laughed, and said, "I do, I do." Then, I had to ask Peggy
Ann to sing 'Dixie', my favorite song:

Oh, I wish I was in the land of cotton,
Old times there are not forgotten,
Look away, look away, look away Dixie Land.

In Dixie Land, where I was born in,
Early on one frosty mornin',
Look away, look away, look away Dixie Land.

I wish I was in Dixie, Hooray! Hooray!
In Dixie Land I'll take my stand
To live and die in Dixie.
Away, away, away down south in Dixie.
Away, away, away down south in Dixie.

Ole Missus marry "Will the weaver"
Willum was a gay deceiver
Look away! Look away! Look away!
Dixie Land

But when he put his arm around 'er,
He smiled fierce as a forty pounder,
Look away! Look away! Look away!
Dixie Land

His face was sharp as a butcher's cleaver
But that did not seem to grieve 'er
Look away! Look away! Look away!
Dixie Land

Ole Missus acted the foolish part
And died for a man that broke her heart
Look away! Look away! Look away!
Dixie Land

Now here's a health to the next ole Missus
An' all the gals that want to kiss us;
Look away! Look away! Look away!
Dixie Land

But if you want to drive 'way sorrow
Come and hear this song tomorrow
Look away! Look away! Look away!
Dixie Land

There's buckwheat cakes and Injun batter,
Makes you fat or a little fatter;
Look away! Look away! Look away!
Dixie Land

Then Hoe it down and scratch your gravel,
To Dixie's Land I'm bound to travel,
Look away! Look away! Look away!
Dixie Land

FRIDAY, APRIL 22, 1864

I had to ask the young lady who was feeding me some delicious chicken soup what day it was. She told me but I found it hard to believe. My recollection of the past several days is hazy, at best. I have only a vague memory of being operated on by Dr. Dempsey. I know he found the bullet but beyond that I am not sure what else he did. Whatever it was I am grateful since I feel so much better.

Miss Peggy Ann, my nurse, is a delight. She helps in every way possible to get a man back on his feet. This morning she told me about her family. It was very moving. Both of her parents suffered violent deaths. Her mother, when a horse kicked her in the head, and her father at Antietam. He was a Union Army officer but decided to go with Lee and the Virginians. She said her cousin Charlotte is here too but I have yet to see her. Their mothers were sisters.

Peggy Ann was trying to teach me all the words to that old song called 'Way Down Upon the Swanee River', a wonderful old tune by Stephen Foster. Never knew but a few of the words before. Now I know them all:

> *'Way down upond de Swanee ribber*
> *Far, far away,*
> *Dere's wha my heart is turning ebber,*
> *Dere's wha de old folks stay.*
> *All up and down de whole creation,*
> *Sadly, I roam,*
> *Still longing for de old*
> *plantation,*
> *And for de old folks at home.*
> *All de world am sad and dreary,*
> *Ebry where I roam.*
> *Oh! darkeys how my heart*
> *grows weary,*
> *Far from de old folks at home.*
> *One little hut among de bushes,*
> *One dat I love,*
> *Still sadly to my mem'ry rushes,*
> *No matter where I rove*
> *When will I see de bees a humming*
> *All round de comb?*
> *When will I hear de banjo tumming*
> *Down in my good old home?*

She is so nice, even gave me a bath with hot wet towels. We had fun singing some of those old songs, like 'Dixie' and 'Battle Hymn of the Republic'. She did most of the singing. I can only hum, although I do know the lyrics to Julia Howe's immortal song. Once again, however, Peggy Ann came to my rescue:

Mine eyes have seen the glory of the coming of the Lord;
He is trampling out the vintage where the grapes of wrath are stored;
He hath loosed the fateful lightning of His terrible swift sword;
His truth is marching on.
Glory! Glory! Hallelujah! Glory! Glory! Hallelujah!
Glory! Glory! Hallelujah! His truth is marching on.

I have seen Him in the watch fires of a hundred circling camps
They have builded Him an altar in the evening dews and damps;
I can read His righteous sentence by the dim and flaring lamps;
His day is marching on.
Glory! Glory! Hallelujah! Glory! Glory! Hallelujah!
Glory! Glory! Hallelujah! His day is marching on.

I have read a fiery Gospel writ in burnished rows of steel;
"As ye deal with My contemners, so with you My grace shall deal";
Let the Hero, born of woman, crush the serpent with His heel,
Since God is marching on.
Glory! Glory! Hallelujah! Glory! Glory! Hallelujah!
Glory! Glory! Hallelujah! Since God is marching on.

He has sounded forth the trumpet that shall never call retreat;
He is sifting out the hearts of men before His judgment seat;
Oh, be swift, my soul, to answer Him! Be jubilant, my feet;
Our God is marching on.
Glory! Glory! Hallelujah! Glory! Glory! Hallelujah!
Glory! Glory! Hallelujah! Our God is marching on.

In the beauty of the lilies Christ was born across the sea,
With the glory in His bosom that transfigures you and me:
As He died to make men holy, let us die to make men free;
While God is marching on.
Glory! Glory! Hallelujah! Glory! Glory! Hallelujah!
Glory! Glory! Hallelujah! While God is marching on.

He is coming like the glory of the morning on the wave,
He is wisdom to the mighty, He is honor to the brave;
So the world shall be His footstool, and the soul of wrong His slave,
Our God is marching on.
Glory! Glory! Hallelujah! Glory! Glory! Hallelujah!
Glory! Glory! Hallelujah! Our God is marching on.

Dr. Dempsey was unaware of Booth's telegraph to Secretary Stanton but was fully aware of Charlotte Parker and her cousin. Booth and Annabelle had gone for a horseback ride around her estate.

"I hope you will forgive me for asking for your help on such short notice Charlotte. I should have written long ago but I just somehow lost your address. My intentions were honorable however so I hope I'll be pardoned for my lapse."

"Well we all know, Patrick, that good intentions pave the road to Hell, but I think we can forgive you this one time. Do you plan to stay in the Army after the war?"

"If we are still here, Charlotte. Unless there are some favorable developments soon, I do not believe the Confederacy will survive. If I do, and the C. S. A. does not, I will probably go into private practice."

"Strange hearing that come from you, a military man."

"What is that?"

"That we are going to lose the war. My daddy is a military man, a major like you, but I never heard him or any of his friends say that."

"How long has it been since you saw your daddy, Charlotte?"

"Well that is true. He has been gone a long time, from the start of hostilities, even before Antietam."

"Whatever is, is Charlotte. What ought to be is a lie. If we lose, we lose, and we will just have to go from there."

Although Dr. Dempsey enjoyed sitting and talking with Charlotte he noticed that Peggy Ann never left my bedside. She seemed to be busy every time he saw her, even out of the corner of his eye, cleaning, or reading to me, or playing some little mind game. Even singing. Charlotte on the other hand, never came upstairs.

Hours passed slowly as everyone except John Surratt took a long afternoon nap. He had decided to take a ride into town and find Powell and Herold. After the fire at McCreed's, they disappeared. Annabelle's huge stable out back held several horses and different kinds of wagons and carriages. A rather elderly Negro gentleman, neatly attired, recommended a small, sporty, horse and carriage that had caught John's eye.

He decided to stop at Shoemaker's photo studio and inquire about his colleagues in crime.

The studio was closed but John decided to try the cellar door. After several hard raps and a few shouts of 'Horace' the door opened a crack. He pushed it open and entered. Horace was drunk, and lying on the cot was a partially dressed Negro woman of uncertain age.

"Just passin' through Horace, trying to find Powell and David."

"Who?"

"Friends of mine and Mr. Booth. They were in that fire at McCreed's."

"Try the tavern at The Virginia Hotel. Booth stays there, so….."

"You having a little party? Looks like fun. Smells like it too."

"You wanna drink? Have a drink. Join the party. Nothing else to do. My business is gone. People are real mad at me now. So many got trapped in that fire and died. When they realized that it was my wife Martha that started it all, the mob and all, they began to blame me. I am guilty. I didn't do it, but I am guilty according to them. So they don't call me anymore. You'll see, when they burn your place down. You're next, so you'll go out of business too. You got a business, John? No, I'm wrong. It's Annabelle's business, or house. A house of ill repute? She's had some great parties there you know. Brings girls in from somewhere for a few days, then they're gone, but we all have a good time while they are here. The girls are expensive but worth it. And Annabelle. She was the most expensive of all."

"Why are they going to burn Annabelle's place?" Surratt asked, pouring another drink.

"Because Lincoln's there. Booth is spreading the word this time. Won't be long. People are getting madder than hell. We got more refugees here than people. They know Grant and his Yankee Doodles are coming to town. Richmond. Rebel Richmond." Horace could hardly stand up, but he kept talking, and Surratt kept listening.

"Booth says his kidnap plot is a failure. The Federals are not going to ransom Lincoln so Lincoln is of no use to him anymore. Wants to kill him, but would rather have a mob do it. Have a little fun you know, with a lynching."

John said goodbye and went on down to the hotel bar. No one was there except Lewis who said nothing about instigating trouble at Annabelle's, but did say that Booth was about finished with Lincoln. "He may want us to peel his ears off in one last try to end the war."

"They might see it our way this time. I will take the picture but this time it will be for real. No fake bandages or somebody else's hand or ears."

"Where did you get that hand last time?" Surratt asked.

"It came from somebody going to get buried. David and I just cut it off. I guess we got the wrong hand Booth says. But, this time we'll get the right ears," Lewis laughed.

All along the way back to Annabelle's place, Surratt went over and over what Horace and Lewis told him about Booth's plans and the distinct possibility that President Lincoln might be disfigured or very likely die. It would be hard to save him from a mob this time, Annabelle being so far out of the center of the city. He thought of his promise to help Booth kidnap the President and of his word and his honor. He had said once before that he had an obligation. But that was to kidnap Lincoln, not to kill him. Besides, he knew that he had come to like the man. He is honest, kind, fair, decent. You ought not kill a man like that, even if you hate what he stands for. That would be wrong. He decided to wait, to see what plans Doc Dempsey might have before saying anything, but not too long.

"Understand you have a lot of guests to handle now and then," John said, smiling at Jessie, the man who got his horse and buggy ready.

"We have a few from time to time. Yes sir." he said, returning the smile and turning away.

"They all pretty Jessie? Or some ugly like me?"

"I am afraid you will have to be the judge of that sir. I wouldn't know one from the other."

"Where they come from?"

"New Orleans. They travel together."

"That so. How long am I going to have to wait for them to come back?"

"Any day now sir. It's been about a month."

"Thank you Jessie. Now you save one or two for me this time. You hear me Jessie?" They both laughed and went about their business. It had been a long day for everyone.

SATURDAY, APRIL 23, 1864

Mamie made bacon and eggs for everybody, but they did not all eat together. Surratt waited for Dr. Dempsey to sit down at the large kitchen table before he pulled out a chair directly across. A few minutes later a still sleepy Peggy Ann joined them.

"Smells great, Mamie," Peggy Ann said, smiling at her breakfast companions.

"Where did you learn to cook?" she asked.

"Don't take much learnin' to do this, Miss Peggy. You got to try my fried catfish. I got a secret batter that will leave your mouth waterin' for my catfish mornin', noon and night."

"Oh, I am looking forward to that" Peggy Ann replied. "Mr. Lincoln seems to be improving, Dr. Dempsey. Temperature and pulse normal. No pain or discomfort. No bowel or urinary difficulties. Do you think he will be all right?"

"With you taking care of him Miss Peggy how could he not?"

"It is not me doctor. It was you who took such good care of him. I would certainly like to have you for my doctor if I should ever need one. You are a very skillful surgeon to have done all you did, and after traveling all night from Richmond to get here. Sergeant Johnson told me all about you."

"It was nothing, Peggy. Really. We have grown used to it during the past three years. Sergeant Johnson and I have stood and worked 'round the clock for 48 hours, two nights in a row, many times. When there is a battle going on you do not have time, no one has time, to rest. That is why I said this was nothing. You get used to it."

"You are far too genuinely modest doctor, for anyone to ever believe you guilty of false modesty."

"Thank you, Peggy. Now tell me, how do you explain your way with people? I know some folks have it and some do not, but you seem to have it in abundance. Such a pleasing personality, I do declare. Now that is an old southern expression I have never used before. How do you like that? I do declare."

"I like it. Now do it again."

"No" he said, laughing. "You are teasing me now."

She just sat there and said not a word. She didn't have to. Her smile said it all.

"What happens next Doc? You and Billy going back to the front? John tried to keep the questions casual, but there was a trace of urgency behind them that Pat Dempsey picked up on.

"I don't know John. Depends on how Mr. Lincoln progresses. So far, as Miss Peggy said, his vital signs look good. If that should continue, I think he will be back on his feet soon, say the next two or three days. It is when I remove the bandages Wednesday morning, the 27th I believe, that we will know if all is well. Now why do you ask? Is there something I should know?"

"Is that when you go back Doc, on Wednesday, if he is well?"

"Yes, I think we could return then. And unless Dr. Mudd wants to stay in the Army he would no doubt come back here. You did not answer my question John. Is there something I should know?"

"It's hard Doc. I don't know what to do, and we ain't got much time, no matter what we decide, or you decide."

Annabelle and Booth entered before Surratt could say any more.

Booth motioned for him to follow him outside the house, where Lewis and David were seated in a small buggy near the stable.

"I want you to go back into town with Herold" Booth said. "This is an emergency John. We have a serious problem with Horace Shoemaker. David will explain it to you. I know Shoemaker respects your judgment, so better you handle this than anyone else. But you must go now. Lewis will take your place here until you get back."

Knowing it would be awkward to attempt to talk with Dr. Dempsey now, Surratt felt he had no choice but to leave with Herold, as Booth directed. They were gone only a few minutes before John realized what the problem with Shoemaker involved, and that there would be no peaceful solution to it. Herold said Horace Shoemaker was once again refusing to participate in any scheme that would injure or disfigure Abraham Lincoln, or any other man. He would not photograph anyone in that predicament, nor allow anyone to use his studio or camera. It was a moral issue, he said, and he told Booth that once before. And now Booth wanted the man's ears cut off. John was expected to talk, or coerce, him into doing it.

The Negro woman on the cot was gone, but Mr. Shoemaker still smelled and acted like he was drunk.

"I know what you want, John, and you are not going to get it," Shoemaker said as soon as he saw David Herold enter the cellar below his studio. "My reputation may be tattered and torn, in the opinion of some of my peers, but it is still intact in my own mind, and that's what counts. To thine own self be true. That's what Shakespeare said, and it's as true today as it was in 1600 or whenever. Ask Booth. Hell, he used to act in Shakespeare's plays. He knows what I mean."

Knowing that he didn't have any chance of changing Horace's mind while at the same time trying to think of how he could get back to talk to Dr. Dempsey.

"I know your business is in bad condition, Horace, because you told me it was. So, how would you feel if Mr. Booth gave you some money, a lot of money maybe, for the use of your studio?"

"I would not accept it."

"Just call it rent. Would you rent the place to somebody if they asked?"

"Not to him."

"Well, suppose a man you do not know said 'I want to rent your studio'. Would you?"

"Maybe but I would say I go with the studio, to see what he is up to, and protect my camera. This is valuable equipment, you know."

"Hey, David" John said after several minutes of silence, "Let's go back to Annabelle's. We ain't doing any good here."

"No. Mr. Booth said stay until it is done even if you have to tie him up or dump him in the river."

John Surratt knew now that it was going to be almost impossible to save Lincoln unless he could reach Dr. Dempsey before he and Billy left Petersburg.

Suddenly he had an idea.

"David, I think I can get Horace to agree to let us use the studio without him being here, but I got to talk to him in private. Understand? You step outside for a smoke while I talk to him about this. I will keep the door open and call you when he agrees, if he agrees."

David Herold thought for a moment, shrugged his shoulders, and left the door open on his way out.

"Mr. Shoemaker," John began slowly and quietly, "I got a way to save your life, and maybe mine, 'cause if we do not do something we are both going to suffer. Booth is a dangerous man and you know David and Lewis will do whatever he orders."

"So get to the point. What do we do?"

David came to the door, looked, but didn't come in.

"We are going to buy some time, Horace, time to give me a chance to get Lincoln out of Petersburg. I am going to get Dr. Dempsey, you know, Major Dempsey, and Billy, his orderly, to take Lincoln back with them. I will tell them about Booth's plans to cut off his ears or let a mob lynch him. Or both. And, if I know Dempsey, he ain't going to like that plan, to murder or mutilate a man."

"Where do I fit in? I don't understand."

"All you have to do Horace, is to tell David when I call him, that you will rent the studio to Mr. Booth no questions asked for one hundred dollars in gold. Rent for only one day, and you will stay away while they are here. I know, it is a lie, but we will have bought time, which is what I need to solve this dilemma."

"I trust John that you won't disappoint me. It is a big gamble for me. I guess for you too. All right. Agreed, I will cooperate. Is that all?"

"That's all Horace. Thank you. David! Horace has agreed to rent the place and stay away while you are here. Tell him Horace. Now let us get out of here, David. I am hungry. You interrupted my breakfast. It was the promise of gold. One hundred dollars in gold is a lot of money, and Shoemaker is as greedy as everybody else I know."

"What makes you think Booth has it, or will pay it?"

"I don't know, or care. That part is up to him don't you see? I got the studio and camera for him. What he pays Shoemaker if anything is up to him alone."

"Never thought of that."

Upon their return, Surratt was surprised and shaken as David drove the wagon to the rear of the house. "Where is the ambulance?" he said aloud, jumping down, running toward the kitchen door. "Where is Dr. Dempsey?"

"He's done gone Mr. John" Mamie said. "Him and Mr. Billy went soon as you all lef' here this mornin'. Some tall feller in a uniform came and got 'em. Said they had to go back right now."

He thought of riding after them, but it would be several hours before he could catch up and return, and during those hours Booth might take Lincoln to the photo studio with Lewis and David. It was too risky. He decided to stay with Lincoln and, once again plan an escape. And he knew that time was working against him.

"Mr. Lincoln I am going to have to move you again. Booth has some ugly ideas of cutting your ears off for a photograph, or throwing you to a lynch mob. I guess the North is not moving fast enough to suit him. I hate telling you this but it is important you know what's happening. How do you feel?"

"I am much better, Mr. Surratt, but Dr. Dempsey did not have time to remove the bandages. They came and got him you know. Must be General Grant is coming. I believe I can move, maybe walk on my own. Where do we go?"

"I don't know yet but it will have to be very soon. I got what he wanted from Shoemaker this morning so he is probably all pumped up for more action. I do not have time to tell you the story now Mr. Lincoln. I have to talk to the girls. They are still here I hope."

"They are, but beware, Miss Charlotte is close to Booth. I believe she wants to be an actress and join his theatrical company. He has made some interesting statements and she is spellbound. Miss Peggy is just the opposite."

"Yes, I have sensed that."

Surratt found Peggy Ann in the stable feeding carrots to the horses and told her what he had learned.

"Give me a moment John. This all comes as news to me. I had no idea of the danger you and Mr. Lincoln are in. But I want to help. Do not say anything about this to cousin Charlotte. It might upset her."

"Take him for a ride in one of Annabelle's carriages Peggy. He says he is well enough to travel and I believe that. Just ask Jessie, the old Negro gentleman who runs the stable for a nice buggy. Do not tell him where you are going, only that your patient needs a little sunlight and fresh air."

"Where am I going?"

"I have an idea but that can wait. When you get out to the road I will be waiting for you. Does that meet with your approval?"

"Whatever you say is all right with me. I am going to get my patient ready for a nice ride in the country now."

"It is a big estate Peggy, so do not let it appear that you are leaving the grounds. Drive around slowly a while, getting closer to the main gate all the time. Follow the sun, that is west, if you get lost. That is where the gate is. I'll be there."

"Thank you John. You are a very smart man."

Back in the house, Surratt put his revolver and holster under his shirt, stuck a few personal things in his pocket and told Mamie he would be outside looking the place over if anyone was trying to find him. He grabbed a few crackers on his way out and started looking for a horse.

It all went well. No one saw either of them as they met at the gate.

"Follow me Peggy. We don't have far to go."

About forty minutes later, Surratt turned off the dirt road toward a large, light brown house with dark brown shutters. It looked abandoned. No other houses could be seen in any direction.

"I think this is it Peggy. I will open the barn now so you drive in and wait. I will come back as soon as I can."

He had to break a window in order to enter Horace Shoemaker's house, but he got in, and promptly left through the back door to the barn. The house needed to be cleaned, but everything was where it should be. Martha Shoemaker was a good housekeeper. But not in her wildest dreams could she have imagined the President of the United States of America, none other than Abraham Lincoln, the bane of her existence, her nemesis, in her home, and in her bed..

"I hope there is something to eat around here" Surratt said, trying to fix the window so that it wouldn't appear broken. "We must not use any candles or lanterns. I know he has neighbors, but I do not want to see any or have them see us. Stay inside."

"I have an idea John. Why don't we get something to eat and rest tonight and tomorrow. Then, as soon as it is dark outside leave the way we came, for my home in Richmond. It too is vacant you know."

And that is what they did. I was made to look like a Negro slave, given a floppy hat that Peggy created, and told to slouch over while driving the carriage. Without a beard, in blackface, big black hat and clothes, I actually looked the part of a humble, obedient slave driving his mistress to her destination. Driving Miss Peggy home.

I relished in the role, as Peggy told me which way to go.

"I cannot believe I am doing this, Peggy Ann. No one will ever believe me," I laughed, "but it seems to work. Every white man should experience what I have seen and done in the past few weeks. Then they would know the true meaning of brotherhood, and equality."

West, and then north, we meandered through the small city of Petersburg, pre-war population 22,000, to the capital of the Confederacy, Richmond. Soldiers were marching everywhere. Refugees flooded the roads to Petersburg and made travel difficult because they were on foot. But we drove on following John on his dappled horse, 'Theresa'. We probably went more than the 24 miles between the two cities, and were all so elated upon arriving at Peggy's house that we just could not contain it. "I hope you have some champagne, or imbibement of some kind to celebrate this, Peggy Ann" John said. "I never thought we would escape them."

Booth was furious. He began accusing Jessie, then Mamie, of withholding information. "Where did they go? When? How? Who was with whom? He wouldn't stop. At one point he pointed his derringer pistol at David and said, "Bring those fools back or you will lie dead among the spring grasses of the Appomattox. Get them. How can I stand this? I want them. I will kill them all. They cannot escape. We will succeed in our quest. Find them and bring them back!"

But, they couldn't find them.

SUNDAY, APRIL 24, 1864

Charlotte Parker spent an inordinate amount of time before a mirror in her bedroom at Annabelle's, brushing her long golden hair before she decided to tell Booth what she thought about cousin Peggy Ann's disappearance.

"She is not like us Mr. Booth. She grew to actually enjoy Lincoln's company, did quite a bit to provide him with comfort."

Charlotte was about to tell Booth where they might be found when Booth exploded yet again: "Yes, and I will kill her too if I find them. Consider her dead and gone, Charlotte dear. She is a traitor!"

Charlotte wasn't ready for that and started to cry. "She is my cousin Mr. Booth."

Attempting to find Lincoln's escape route, Lewis and David knocked on the door of every house on Sycamore Road, both north and south of Annabelle's place for a distance. No one had seen any strangers in the area. Upon seeing the broken window in one home and no one there to answer the door, both men decided to enter the house. On the kitchen table was a note addressed to Mr. Shoemaker thanking him for the use of his home, though without his permission.

> "I would like to come and visit you some day when the war is over. I know you are a loyal American. I would consider it an honor were you to write to me about your late wife, Martha. She was a lovely woman.
>
> With my kindest regards, I am
> And, it was signed A. Lincoln.

Powell put the note in his pocket and the two of them went back to see their leader, John Wilkes Booth.

The Richmond Dispatch, 'Best Newspaper in Virginia', carried a long front page story about President Jefferson Davis speaking out in favor of the kidnapping of his counterpart to the north, "that high stakes gambler willing to sacrifice the lives of so many thousands of innocent men and boys to further the cause of northern industrialists bound and determined to wreck all southern opposition and competition."

He railed against those misguided few who control the Yankee press and want the South to abandon its culture, its freedom to enjoy the fruits of its labor, and slavery.

Davis said "We look forward to vindication and reparations for all the damage inflicted by Lincoln's aggressions, though he may not live to see it. John Wilkes Booth has done us a great service. Somewhere in Virginia, at this very moment Abraham Lincoln is cowering in his grave-to-be. He may not live another day unless the Federal Government in Washington declares a cease fire, an immediate end to hostilities."

"We may need some protection, Peggy. Should Booth learn from Charlotte where you live in Richmond, in the event they guess that we may have come here for refuge, then he or Lewis and David, would be dispatched to do us great harm, to kill us all."

"Cousin Charlotte would never do that John. She is my kin."

"You may be correct, Peggy Ann, but we cannot gamble. Booth could force her to reveal your address if she does not cooperate with him, or he could find it some other way. I think he or Annabelle knows your surname. The rest is easy."

"Who will protect us John? I just read the 'Dispatch' story about Mr. Davis and his liking for Mr. Booth's kidnap plan. I don't believe he would provide much protection. I would sooner ask Dr. Dempsey."

"That is what I intend to do. If I can telegraph him he might be able to help."

Surratt found the military telegraph office at the capitol, but was promptly told that he should talk to the provost marshal if he wanted to reach Dr. Dempsey or any other military officer or installation. "Ask Colonel Macon," the desk sergeant told him. "He is the only one who can approve that."

John sensed that he would have to have a convincing story to gain approval, that there would be no second chance. "Colonel Macon, my name is John Post. I have to send a telegraph to Major Patrick Dempsey, a surgeon on General Lee's staff. General Lee's brother, Mr. Albert Lee, whom I care for here in Richmond, is in dire need of protection from Annabella, a disease he contracted when his brother, General Robert E. Lee was here last, and asked for help on an emergency basis, before Annabella or any of its related ailments could kill Albert and others, including Miss Peggy, his sister, and me."

"I did not know that General Lee had a brother, or sister, Mr. Post. And you say they both live here, in Richmond?"

"My family and I take care of them, Colonel; my wife and I have known the family for years. We are all close friends."

"You certainly may telegraph Major Dempsey, Mr. Post. And, if my office can help you or General Lee's family I will do whatever you ask."

At the request of Major General George B. McClellan, projected Democrat nominee for President of the United States in November, 1864, Roger Taney, the Republican Chief Justice of the United States Supreme Court, and very much in sympathy with McClellan's pledge to end the war if elected, issued a statement that immediately made the front page of newspapers nationwide.

On the basis of legislation passed by Congress notice is hereby given that the Office of President of the United States will be declared vacant as of 12 o'clock Friday night, April 29th, 1864 unless occupied by President Abraham Lincoln in person by that time. Absent Mr. Lincoln, Vice President Hannibal

Hamlin will be sworn in as president. While the Constitution of the United States of American is silent on this issue, this court may find the situation, though no fault of Mr. Lincoln, can no longer be tolerated. The people have a right to know that we have a bona fide Head of State no matter the cause or reason for his vacancy after 30 days.

> Roger Taney
> Chief Justice
> United States Supreme Court

McClellan was elated. He would not have to run against Lincoln, probably never see him again. Most people agreed. It was all over. Abraham Lincoln was probably dead.

John waited for a reply, first in Colonel Henry Macon's office, then on a bench outside the old customs building, now the capitol of the Confederacy. Hours passed. There wasn't anything more he could do. He knew they were all at the end of the rope. He smiled at his own macabre joke, but stopped when he found himself looking at the branches of nearby trees.

He was about to leave when Colonel Macon hailed him.

"Mr. Post. I have a telegraph for you. From Major Dempsey."

"Urgent you bring Albert and Miss Peggy here soon as possible. This is a private matter and must be kept confidential. Use whatever wagon Army can supply for transportation. Take Brook Road north from Richmond until you reach Telegraph Road. Continue north on Telegraph Road toward Hanover Junction.

We will intercept when appropriate.

Major Patrick Dempsey,
C. S. A. Medical Corps"

"Where can I find a large enclosed wagon Colonel?"

"I may have one here Mr. Post. Follow me. I will order my deputy to bring you one."

"Here."

"Yes, here. Give me a few minutes."

And that's all it took. Surratt had a large Army wagon used by the provo marshal office, and marked accordingly.

"I'll see that it is returned to you as soon as practicable. Thank you for your assistance sir. I am certain General Lee will appreciate your kindness. I will certainly make it known to him. Goodbye."

John, Peggy Ann and I packed some of Peggy's belongings, some food and blankets, and left to find Dr. Dempsey and, hopefully, safety. Peggy Ann lived at the corner of Franklin and 1st Street. But for a turn at the end of the street, we would have seen, and been seen, by Booth, Lewis and David. Charlotte had decided that Booth would never kill anyone, and she really wanted a stage career.

Peggy and I sat in the back of the wagon as John drove the team of horses through the now heavily populated streets of Richmond. People seemed to know war was coming and had boarded up their windows everywhere. Confederate infantry and cavalry stood at ease or in parade formation at almost every intersection. Traffic was thick and hurried, but no one stopped us.

"I said I wanted to stop in for a chat with President Davis but I did not think that would be wise under the circumstances. I wonder what he would have said."

"Might have asked you for a job, or an appointment when this is over. Looks like it may be over soon."

"I hope so. But I fear the worst. There will be a lot to do when it is all over, so Jeff Davis need not worry. Reconstruction will keep him, and the others, and us, occupied for years. We will have to rebuild, and I want to be sure that is done right. Otherwise we will have won the war but the South will have won the peace, and that will take generations to overcome."

Surratt was moving the wagon right along the Telegraph Road, north toward Hanover Junction when he noticed a particularly large Confederate cavalry unit approaching. A distinguished looking gentleman in full dress grey uniform raised his hand to signal him to stop.

"You have received a message from Major Dempsey?"

"I have."

"Then you should know that I am General Robert E. Lee. With your permission sir, I shall escort you and your party through our front lines, at which time, under flag of truce, you will entrain and continue on a short distance to the enemy lines where you will be received by General Grant or his officers. From that time on you and your party will be guests of the United States Army of the Potomac. I have asked one of the newspaper reporters to communicate as directly as possible with General Grant and Secretary of War

Stanton, so I am confident you will be in good hands for the remainder of your journey."

"Please inform Mr. Lincoln, for whom I still have the highest regard, that I did not have any knowledge, or anything to do with his kidnapping. I think Mr. Booth is insane, and apologize for his criminal behavior on behalf of the Confederacy. Now let us get on with the business at hand."

We did not see each other or speak, although I heard every word and Lee knew it. It was as if he had been speaking directly to me all the while.

Several lanterns illuminated the small railroad station at Hanover Junction, Virginia, where the Virginia Central Railroad and Richmond, Fredericksburg & Potomac Railroad cross. I believe it was about 8 p.m. when we arrived at the terminal building. Except for the dozen or so Confederate cavalrymen who remained mounted, there was no one else to be seen. It was very quiet, eerie, well under control. I believe General Lee wanted it that way and issued orders cordoning off the entire junction. He was probably as much afraid of what his troops might see and hear and do as he was of ours.

I could hear and see the train itself, which consisted only of a steam engine and passenger car. The steam and lighting and men in uniform on horseback made an unforgettable scene.

A high ranking officer on General Lee's staff dismounted, introduced himself, and asked that we follow him to the train. Large white sheets serving as flags of truce were affixed to each side of the engine's cowcatcher and rear of the passenger car.

As Major General James, the Confederate Provost Marshal who had been assigned as my escort officer, and I sat opposite each other, the train began to move out. Mr. Surratt and Miss Post were seated across from us.

General James said that the train would continue on through the Confederate lines to a predetermined point where a Union officer would take back the train and he, James, would alight. That is all he said, and that is the way it happened.

In a few minutes the train stopped, James left, and a youthful Major General George A. Custer entered the car. He saluted, smiled and sat down where a Rebel general had been seated moments ago. I was so happy and proud to see that blue uniform again, that I just could not control the tears that followed.

Custer said that General Grant would meet us at the railroad station in Fredericksburg and then return to his headquarters. So too would Custer. Admiral David Porter would also meet us at Fredericksburg and escort us to the end of the line, at Aquia Creek, where the Naval gunboat BAT would carry us home via the Potomac River, to Washington City, and Mary.

Lieutenant General Ulysses S. Grant greeted me with a firm handshake, a smile, and a few tears in his eyes. "You cannot imagine how happy I am to see you again, Mr. President. It has only been since March 8th as I recall, but it seems a lifetime."

"I share your thoughts, General. It was a lifetime."

Grant told me about Justice Taney's edict and the obvious necessity to hurry. He said it could and would be done, but no time should be wasted. And, it wasn't. I arrived on time and am glad to be home. If only everyone in this war could be as fortunate as I am boys, and get to go home when it is all over.

FRIDAY, APRIL 29, 1864

Word of Lincoln's survival and pending arrival at the Capitol this morning, was greeted with an enormous sigh of collective relief. By the thousands, people gathered in front of the Capitol Building and along Maryland Avenue to 7th Street, and south on 7th to the wharves. to see and cheer Abraham Lincoln, their President. You know, the man from Illinois.

EPILOGUE

President Lincoln and his wife Mary Todd Lincoln were reunited, and the war continued on.

John Wilkes Booth was never apprehended. He assassinated Lincoln on April 14, 1865, escaped for a few days, and was killed in a barn, in Virginia, April 26, 1865.

The conspirators were hung.

Robert Shoemaker was killed by David Herold who reasoned that Shoemaker must have told John Surratt that his home on Sycamore Road, in Petersburg, was available as a hideout.

John Surratt, Jr. was pardoned by President Lincoln and had nothing to do with the assassination. Lincoln tried to give Surratt some of the reward money but Edwin Stanton said no. John Surratt died in 1916.

Dr. Samuel Mudd was also pardoned by President Lincoln. He too had helped save the President's life. His misfortune in helping J. W. Booth to escape caused him to be imprisoned in Florida for several years.

Dr. Patrick Dempsey married Peggy Ann Post and purchased Annabelle's house with the reward money they were given for their part in President Lincoln's recovery and return. Dr. Dempsey was given $100,000.00 and Miss Post $25,000.00. They had six children and lived happily ever after.

Annabelle White moved to New Orleans where she became very successful, as well as infamous, as the sole proprietor of the most exclusive bordello in Southern Louisiana, The Governor's Club. Membership by invitation only.

Miss Charlotte Parker became one of Annabelle's most popular residents.

Major General George B. McClellan, Democrat candidate for President, was defeated by Abraham Lincoln in November, 1864, thanks largely to Major General William T. Sherman having taken Atlanta on September 3.

Angus McCreed's son, also an undertaker, was given $25,000.00 in honor of the help his father had given the President, and started a new business in Petersburg after the war.

Edwin M. Stanton died in 1869.

Jefferson Davis was imprisoned at Fortress Monroe for many years after the war. He wrote "The Rise and Fall of the Confederate Government", while in solitary confinement. The last years of his life were spent in his home overlooking the Gulf of Mexico in Biloxi, Mississippi. He died in 1889.

Robert E. Lee died in 1870.

Ulysses S. Grant was elected President of the United States in 1868 and 1872.

Over 600,000 men were killed in the Civil War; 260,000 Confederates, one of every ten white men in the south, and 364,000 Unionists, including 37,000 Negroes. Of the 400,000 men wounded many would die young. Over one million casualties.

"The only way to win a war is to prevent it."
Secretary of State George C. Marshall

BIBLIOGRAPHY

Atlas to Accompany the Official Records of the Union and Confederate Armies, compiled by Captain Calvin Cowles, 23rd U. S. Infantry. Washington, D. C. Government Printing Office 1891 - 1895.

Manhunt: The Twelve Day Chase for Lincoln's Killer. James Swanson, 2006 Harper Collins Publishers, N.Y. 10022

Grant and Sherman: The Friendship That Won the Civil War. Charles B. Flood, 2005. Farrar, Straus and Giroux Publishers.

Come Retribution: The Confederate Secret Service and the Assassination of Lincoln. Wm. A. Tidwell with James O. Hall and David W. Gaddy, published by Barnes & Noble, Inc., by arrangement with the University Press of Mississippi, 1997.

Team of Rivals: The Political Genius of Abraham Lincoln. Doris Kearns Goodwin, 2005. Simon & Schuster, Publisher, N.Y. 10020.

Battle Cry of Freedom: The Civil War. James M. McPherson. Oxford University Press, N. Y. 1988.

Lincoln. David Herbert Donald, 1995. First published in the United Kingdom by Jonathan Cape, Random House, London.

ACKNOWLEDGEMENTS

Abraham Lincoln's favorite poem was titled <u>Mortality</u>, or <u>Oh, Why Should the Spirit of Mortal Be Proud</u>? The author was William Knox (1789 - 1825).

<u>Battle Hymn of the Republic</u> was written by Julia W. Howe, in 1861, to the tune of <u>John Brown's Body</u>.

<u>Dixie</u> was written by Daniel Decatur Emmett of Mt. Vernon, Ohio and premiered in September 1859. It was Lincoln's favorite song.

<u>Way Down Upon the Swanee River</u> was written by Stephen Foster.

I wish to thank the Library of Virginia, Richmond, Virginia, for their generous help with maps and other issues.

Also, the Virginia Historical Society in Richmond, Virginia for their help with the same issues and maps, particularly of roads and railroads in 1864.

And for his help and advice I thank Mr. Tom Mueller, a research librarian at the Citrus County Library, Inverness, Florida, especially for finding a Civil War atlas that was helpful in understanding battle lines in the spring of 1864.

I want to thank the New York Times for reprints of articles which appeared in their newspaper in 1864 and 1865.

Thanks also to Mrs. George (Dianne) Bilodeau, for her patience, advice, and computer typing skills. She made this book happen.

And, finally, to my wife of 54 years, Shirley, my three daughters, Eileen, Diane and Sheila for their editorial comments, and to my son Paul N. Herbert who has researched and written a wide variety of Civil War articles for the Washington Times, and other newspapers in and around Fairfax, Virginia, for many years. Thank you.

ABOUT THE AUTHOR

V. A. (Victor Albert) Herbert, born in Springfield, Mass., August 4, 1928, attended public schools and graduated Boston University (BS in BA) in 1950, and the University of Akron (MBA) in 1970.

A life-long amateur historian who has lived and traveled extensively in southern states during his 35 year association with the Goodyear Tire & Rubber Co., the Upjohn Company and the U. S. Air Force, Mr. Herbert's library of 2300 books include many novels and non-fictionalized accounts of the civil war.

A veteran of the Korean War (61st Fighter Squadron), Mr. Herbert's additional duty assignment as the squadron's Public Information Officer, followed his tenure as a speech writer for the Commanding General of the Air Training Command, in Illinois.

Mr. Herbert has served the nation as an Air Force officer (1950 - 1954), his state (Ohio), as the Assistant Director of Commerce (1972 - 1974), his county (Summit), as one of three at-large County Commissioners (1967-1972), and his city (Akron), as one of three Councilman-At-Large (1964 - 1966). As a Democrat councilman, he introduced and helped pass the first anti-polygraph law and toughest fair housing ordinance in the nation.

Currently retired, Mr. Herbert and his wife, Shirley, have spent summers in Ohio and winters in Florida since 2000.

Their son, Paul N. Herbert, has researched and written Civil War articles for the Washington Times and other weekly newspapers in Virginia for several years.